CTR's ring

To the staff at Line Upon Line!
    Thanks for all you guys do!
Remember, its always a good idea
to choose the right.

        ♡ Melissa Clegett

CTR's ring

Melissa Ann Aylstock

Bonneville Books
Springville, Utah

ISBN: 1-55517-833-2
e.1

Published by Bonneville Books
Imprint of Cedar Fort Inc.
www.cedarfort.com

Distributed by:

Typeset by Natalie Roach
Cover design by Nicole Williams
Cover design © 2005 by Lyle Mortimer

Printed in the United States of America
10 9 8 7 6 5 4 3 2 1

Printed on acid-free paper

Dedication

For my children's friends everywhere—especially CS and MA. How fortunate I am that they have been willing to share their lives freely with me despite the years between us.

Acknowledgments

I wish to thank Roger for his love and tireless answering of the same basic computer questions day after day. I also wish to thank Brittany, whose eager anticipation of each new chapter pushed me to finish this book. And, of course, I thank Chris, who wears his CTR ring everyday–even in Iraq.

TABLE OF CONTENTS

SATURDAY

*C*ameron Richards yelped in annoyance. The hammer missed its intended mark and struck him on a finger instead. He shook his hand rapidly and muttered at the undercarriage of his Jeep. He had to roll over twice to retrieve the hammer he had thrown. The next time he hit the U-joint, it was with better precision.

"You dirty dog, let go!" Cameron yelled at the part.

With a metallic pop, the last piece of the fractured U-joint broke free and skidded across the gravel embankment. What was his mother thinking, having him drive all the way to California to meet this paternal grandmother whom he had never even heard of until last year?

Cameron wiped oil-streaked hands on his faded jeans. He grabbed onto the rear bumper and pulled his six-foot frame out from under the scratched, green Wrangler that was currently dead on the shoulder of Interstate 80 in Roseville, California. He shook his head vigorously, and dust and gravel flew out of his dark, wavy hair. He pushed a lock of it out of his eyes; he was in need of a haircut. Pulling a pair of cheap sunglasses down over his nose, he hid his velvet blue eyes. He was a long way from home, and he was tired, hungry, and frustrated.

He kicked the knobby tires on his lifted rig in annoyance, and dirt went flying. It wasn't that replacing the U-joint was difficult; it was just one more thing. He almost wished he had a cigarette. He sighed heavily and started walking toward the Douglas Boulevard exit, looking for an auto parts store and food.

He saw fast food establishments close to the freeway but passed them by. The walk was calming him down. A block ahead he saw Mel's Diner advertising "old-fashioned" food. He decided food would energize him, so he made that his target. The parking lot was crowded. It was a good sign.

Cameron entered the restaurant and caught the eye of the afternoon hostess. On her nametag was a neatly typed "Lauren."

"Hi. How many?"

"Just one. Smoking, please."

"We don't have a smoking section."

"What? Well, where do the smokers go to eat?" he asked in sincere puzzlement.

She smiled and pointed outside.

"You're kidding."

"No. You can't smoke in restaurants in California. Actually, you can't smoke anywhere indoors in California . . . like at work and stuff."

"Whoa, are you sure?"

"Of course I'm sure. I live here. You must be new. Where are you from?" Lauren asked.

"Up until last week, Fargo, North Dakota. Before that, Kentucky. That's where I grew up."

"Well, do you want to try eating without the smoke?" Lauren grinned at him.

"Nonsmoking is fine. I was just surprised—you say this is all restaurants?" he asked, still amazed.

Her ponytail bobbed as she nodded.

"Okay, table for one—no smoking please."

Lauren smiled and her green eyes sparkled with amusement. She walked toward a booth near the front window and handed him a menu. He reached out his left hand to take it, and the black and turquoise CTR ring on his index finger caught her eye. Her eyes narrowed a bit, and he caught the change in her expression.

"What?"

"Why do you smoke anyway?" she said with mild disdain in her voice.

"Huh?"

"I mean, I can't believe you wear your ring while you smoke cigarettes. Don't you find that a bit hypocritical?"

He looked down at his ring and then back at her. "What are you talking about? What does my ring have do to with smoking?"

"Duh! CTR." When he continued to look confused, she added in a slow, parental voice. "Choose the Right."

"Choose the right what? I don't understand," he said, genuinely perplexed.

Now Lauren was the one who was confused. She looked at his ring, then at him, then at his ring. "You have on a CTR ring. The ring you first got in Primary?" Her words came out more a question than a statement.

"Primary?" He looked down at his ring, which he had been wearing for over a year. "I found this ring at the gas station I worked at in Fargo. Someone left it on the sink in the bathroom. When no one came back to claim it, I started wearing it because it had my initials on it—Cameron T. Richards. It fit and I liked how it looked."

At this news Lauren became positively red-faced. "Oh my gosh, I am so sorry."

"Sorry for what?"

Lauren reached out and touched his index finger. Her hand was cool and welcome on his rough skin. "I thought you were a member of the Church. I mean a member of my Church. This ring," and she tapped her finger on his CTR ring for emphasis, "is something that we get right before we're baptized. It's to remind us to choose the right. A sort of gentle reminder to follow Christ. I shouldn't have given you such a hard time about the smoking." She shook her head. "Clearly you're not a Mormon."

At the word Mormon, Cameron jerked his hand away. "Mormon? You're a Mormon?" He blurted out the words.

"Uh-huh." She lowered her voice. "I'm a member of The Church of Jesus Christ of Latter-day Saints—or 'Mormon,' which is probably how we are known by most people outside the Church."

"And this ring?" he said holding his hand out toward her. "Is this a 'Mormon' ring?"

She nodded and held out her right hand to show him her ring. Cameron looked at her hand. On it was a silver ring surrounded by Noah's ark animals. Upon closer inspection Cameron could see the familiar crest he wore on his finger—the initials CTR imbedded in the polished silver.

"Oh brother." He tugged at his CTR ring and pulled it off his finger. It left a white band of sun-starved skin exposed. He held the ring in his left hand and inspected it. "I always loved this ring too. Really, what were the chances someone would leave a ring that had my initials on it? I never for a moment thought it was anything other than that. But now I can't wear it—I'm a Christian."

Lauren took in a slow, deliberate breath. Her face reddened. Slowly letting her chest fall, she looked this stranger directly in the eyes. "I'm also a Christian."

Cameron shook his head in the negative. "I don't think so. You're Mormon. Everyone knows Mormons aren't Christian."

Lauren looked at the big clock in the restaurant and then back at Cameron. "Listen, you need to eat, and I need to get back to work. But tell you what, I'm off in ten minutes. If you want, I'll come back and talk to you . . . or not, it's up to you."

Cameron thought this over. "Well, I *am* new in town and would like the company—sure, if you don't mind. But I can tell you right now, I'm not interested in joining your church."

Lauren smiled slowly and patiently at Cameron. He met her gaze. Her teeth were straighter and whiter than those of any girl he had ever seen. Her eyes were a brilliant sea green. The combination actually made Cameron weak in the knees. Of course, it could also be the twelve-hour ride in the Jeep.

"I understand." She said softly, the tone in her voice much less agitated than before. "I'm not going to try to convert you, if that's what you think." She turned and walked back to the front.

Within a minute a pleasant looking girl tagged "Brianna" approached his table to take his order. The first thing he noticed was that she was wearing a smaller, pink version of his CTR ring. He looked around the restaurant to see if everyone in the restaurant had one on.

As he waited for his order, Cameron watched Lauren. She was pleasant to watch—very pretty. Her pale blond hair was not so long, so her ponytail bounced as she walked people to their table. Her complexion was clear, her lashes were long, and her eyelids were carefully accented by a dusting of smoky shadow. Her lips were full and tinted with pink sparkly stuff. She was amazingly good-looking. Too bad she was a Mormon.

If he weren't careful, he would find himself feeling bad about how abrupt he had been with her. He had to remind himself that she was the one who had started this whole thing over the smoking issue. He also had to admit that she was a person of convictions by the way she had called him on it. He admired that. He half smiled. It was ironic that she had picked up on the one bad habit he was actually trying to break. She didn't know that when he had asked for the smoking section—it was only out of habit. He hadn't smoked for months.

Brianna set down his order. She efficiently poured him a cup of coffee. When he was about halfway through his burger and "Melfries," Lauren returned. She slid onto the black, padded seat across from him.

She looked him straight in the eyes, catching him a little off guard. "First, I want to apologize for my rudeness. I never meant to pry, and it is none of my business if you smoke—even if you were a member of our church. Second . . ."

Cameron held his right hand up in the air to stop her. "Let me respond to the 'first' first. Apology accepted, and I don't smoke anymore. I stopped a few months ago . . . too expensive actually. I think I may have mentioned I came from Kentucky."

Lauren nodded.

"Kentucky is a tobacco state—everyone smokes—it's no big deal. Well, actually, it used to not be a big deal. It is now. I asked for the smoking section out of habit, I suppose. Most all of my friends still smoke—even the ones in North Dakota. Also, I'm a bit tired. I've been on the road all day, and I wasn't thinking. Okay, you can go on with 'second.'"

Lauren regarded him thoughtfully now. His eyes were clear, and his wind-tossed, dark hair curled up around his forehead. His hands were rough but strong. She spoke more quietly now. "Well, second . . . I had a few minutes to think about our last conversation. I think I could sense you have some bad feelings where 'Mormons' are concerned. The last thing I want to do is add to that. I thought I could just keep you company until you are on your way again. We won't even talk about church—either mine or yours, okay?"

"Not okay." But he had a smile on his face as he said it. He picked up the ring that had been sitting next to his coffee. He turned it back and forth between his finger and his thumb. "Since I've been wearing this ring for over a year, I think I may want to ask some questions about it and its 'Mormon' meaning." He put the ring on the tip of his index finger and stared at it for a while.

Lauren sat patiently, waiting for his question.

When she didn't respond, he spoke again. His voice was low, and Lauren leaned forward slightly to hear him better. "I have to admit there was always something about this ring that intrigued me. I wondered why the guy who owned it had his name in a crest . . . and what the inscription inside meant."

When Lauren looked puzzled, he handed her the ring. On the inside curve of the size twelve ring, in block letters, was written "WORTH THE DRIVE." Lauren smiled.

"What? What does it mean?"

"Well, I can't say for certain, but my guess is that this was a gift from a girlfriend, or wife, to the person who left it. My aunt engraved the same thing in my uncle's wedding ring."

"Why?"

"Oh, my aunt and uncle met at a church dance, but he lived in the San Fernando Valley, and she lived in the South Bay."

Cameron looked confused.

Lauren laughed, "Oh, sorry, those are areas in southern California, and they're about forty, tough Los Angeles freeway miles apart. My uncle used to make the drive a couple times a week to take out my aunt; eventually they got married. She always told him she was 'worth the drive.' He hated the drive but obviously not my aunt. Anyway, she had that engraved in his wedding band. I think it's kind of sweet."

"Well, that's as good an explanation as anything. Anyway, not knowing any of its history, and in light of the fact that no one came to claim it, I just wore it because it had my initials on it."

Lauren handed the ring back to Cameron. "What's your name?"

"Cameron Thomas Richards—C.T.R."

"Nice name."

"Thanks." He reached out across the table and tapped the small CTR ring on her finger. "Do you think about being a Mormon when you wear your ring?"

She pulled her hand back a bit and blushed. "I suppose, but I've worn this ring for so long that I sometimes take its meaning for granted. That is totally bad on my part, but it just happens. I think after today, at least for a while, I will probably think more about what this ring is supposed to represent."

"What *does* it represent?"

"Well, choosing the right, of course. But for me it's more about being a daughter of God. In our church—and I'm just guessing that you don't know that much about Mormons—we take being sons and daughters of God pretty literally. We are taught to develop a close relationship with our Heavenly Father through Christ. As far as your other question, I can't speak for everyone in our church, but my guess is that most Mormons don't think about being 'Mormon.' That's just what people started calling us because we have the Book of Mormon. We really do think more in terms of being Heavenly Father's children."

"Okay, so that brings up another topic. I already know about your 'Golden Bible,' but to be honest, I was always a bit surprised at how much attention it got at church."

"So what church is that?"

"Oh, all of them."

"But what denomination?"

"Christian."

"No, I mean like what sect? Baptist, Methodist, Assembly of God?"

"It depended on where we lived. Sometimes Baptist, but my mom liked the Methodists better. The Assembly of God folks were nice but really intense. Mostly we would just go to the closest Christian church. In the summer though, me and my sister would go to all of the Christian churches in town. Mom would find every Bible school around and send us—kind of like free summer camp. I didn't mind, though; it beat hanging out at home." Cameron smiled and shook his head at the thought of all the churches he had been to in his life.

"Okay. That is just an odd concept for me to think about. In my church we change buildings when we move, but not religions." Lauren tapped her clean, short nails on the table.

"I guess we don't think about it as changing religions. They are all basically Christian churches, and that would be my religion. Anyway, back to the 'Golden Bible.' What is it really—I mean, what does a Mormon say it is? I already know what other Christians think of it: 'It's the work of the devil.'" Cameron shook his head and laughed as he mimicked the pastors he had heard.

"Ouch! I know that's what some people think. It makes me crazy that people outside our church want to define us without getting to know us. But as to what the Book of Mormon is, that's easy—it's a second witness to Christ's ministry here on earth. After his death he visited his 'other sheep.' You've read that in the New Testament, right? Anyway, he taught people outside of Jerusalem, and they wrote the record that was later translated."

"I thought some guy named Joe Smith wrote the book."

"No, *Joseph* Smith just *translated* it."

"From what language? Who wrote it?"

"Basically, four prophets who lived in ancient America wrote it. It appeared to be Egyptian hieroglyphics inscribed on plates of gold."

"Okay, so that's where the 'Golden Bible' comes from. But why would ancient Americans write in Egyptian hieroglyphics—and where is this 'Golden Bible' now?"

"I don't know if I have time to answer the first question because I have to leave pretty soon, but as far as the second question goes, no one really knows. After it was translated, the Lord hid it up."

"Well, that's convenient," Cameron said with a touch of sarcasm. "And you believe all this?"

Lauren looked Cameron straight in the eyes. "With all my heart," she testified.

Her piercing look caught Cameron off guard. He could sense a change in the air—a charged feeling. He could almost feel an electric rush through his body.

Lauren didn't avert her gaze, so Cameron looked away to break the intense connection.

Looking down, he said, "Listen, I didn't mean to offend you. Obviously, there is a lot I don't know about your church. To my knowledge, you are the first Mormon I have ever met. Thing is, I'm already a Christian, so even if your church were a Christian church—and I don't know if I am willing to even believe that based on one conversation with one pretty Mormon girl—I don't need more

Christian churches in my life."

Lauren blushed when Cameron said "pretty Mormon girl." She paused for a moment and then said, "I understand, but maybe someday something will happen to you and you'll remember this conversation and think that maybe the Mormon Church isn't all that bad. Maybe you'll say to yourself, 'Hey, I met this Mormon girl once and she was okay—normal even.'"

A horn honked twice outside the restaurant and Lauren sighed. "I hate it when she does that."

"What? The lady in that minivan out there?"

"Yeah, that 'lady' is my mom."

"Oops. No offense intended. She looks like a nice lady in a minivan."

Lauren laughed. "She is. I just hate it when she honks for me at the restaurant. It makes me feel about five. Listen, I have to go, but you have a good life, okay?"

"You too Lauren the Mormon." He smiled.

"I plan to." Lauren smiled back confidently as she walked toward the front door.

Cameron paid his bill and walked back toward his truck, wondering where he was going to find a U-joint, but luck was with him. Not far from Mel's he saw a Napa Auto Parts store. He headed there and bought the ten-dollar item that looked more like an X than a U. He grabbed a Coke from the machine out front and headed back toward the freeway. Kicking rocks along the side of the boulevard was a mild diversion as he trudged up the off-ramp toward his truck.

Luckily, he hadn't needed much more than a hammer and a socket to take off the old U-joint and put on the new one. He loved his Jeep for this very reason. It was a simple vehicle to fix by himself. Working at the gas station had taught him to do almost everything he would ever need to do to keep his Jeep running. The pay was lousy, but the experience was worth it. He hoped to get a job in the service department of a car dealership in or near Roseville.

With the Jeep fixed, he rummaged through the glove box for the crude map his mother had sent with him. He read "Douglas Boulevard exit" in his mother's tight, small handwriting. He hadn't realized that he was so close to his grandmother's. He pulled onto the freeway only to get off three hundred yards ahead.

He still wasn't sure why his mother had insisted he come here. Sure his mother had told him his grandmother had fallen and hurt her wrist, and he knew she needed help, but why him? This was his father's mother, and Cameron hadn't even known she existed until after his father had died. She had never bothered to be a part of his life, never tried to find their family, so why should he be in hers now?

After three tries Cameron finally found Washington Boulevard. His mother's directions left something to be desired, and the fact that this town changed the name of their streets every time you crossed an intersection didn't help much. Reading from his mother's hastily penned note, crushed under his hand on his steering wheel, he turned left on Main Street, left on Cedar, and right on Ash.

At eight o'clock in the evening, the sun was just setting. It was warm, but nothing like the Nevada desert had been earlier in the day. He pulled up across the street from Clara Thelma Richards's home, according to the address on his paper, and sat for a moment to take in the surroundings. The houses were small, older homes, with wooden clapboard siding. Most of the homes, while sporting a variety of colors, had white trim. His grandmother's was no exception. The pale blue paint on the home was a bit faded but clean. The white trim had a high gloss and looked freshly painted. The lawn was cropped close and edged. An older, metal oscillating sprinkler was set toward the front of the lawn. Every thirty seconds the arched spray watered the sidewalk and the small, red Honda parked in front of the house. Cameron was a little surprised at all of this because his mother had said that his grandmother had broken her wrist in a recent fall and could use some help taking care of things around the house. He had assumed that house and lawn maintenance were going to be part of his duties.

As he pondered this, the front door opened, and three women stepped out. The oldest of the three crossed the covered porch and started to make her way down the steps. One of the other women said something to her, and the older woman stopped and turned to go back to the porch. Then the younger of the three women went down the steps and dashed around the side of the house while the sprinkler was in its frontal position. In a few seconds, the water stopped its graceful arching and slowly receded back toward the sprinkler. That done, the two younger women walked toward the Honda, climbed in, and pulled away from the curb as the older woman stood smiling and waving.

Cameron grabbed the roll bar for support and slid himself down from the Jeep. The older woman stopped her waving hand in mid-air to watch as he crossed the street. She looked at him with what appeared to Cameron to be astonishment. He hesitated for a moment. What if he wasn't expected today? *Oh well, here I am, Gramma, ready or not*, he thought, as he ascended the steps to the porch.

"Cameron?" The older woman spoke first.

Cameron nodded his head. "I hope this was the day you were expecting me."

"Oh yes, yes, but my gosh, I knew you looked like the Richards's side of the family, but I can't believe how much you actually look like your grandfather. You're so tall. Much taller than your father. The resemblance to your grandfather is remarkable. Your father always took after my side of the family, but my goodness, you certainly have the Richards's side in you."

"I don't think I've ever seen a picture of my grandfather—you either, for that matter. This whole thing is a bit odd for me." He looked down at her wrists. She had an ace bandage on one, but not the cast he was expecting. "How is your arm, or wrist? Mother said you broke it."

"I didn't actually break it, thank goodness. It was more of a bad sprain, which the doctor said is worse than a break for pain. It only hurts now when I try to lift things or turn it in a certain way. That's why I still wear this." She raised her left hand for emphasis. "To remind me not to overdo it. Come. Come in the house. I have supper waiting for you."

"Sounds good." Cameron gulped nervously and followed his grandmother into her home. He was not hungry after leaving Mel's Diner, but he knew he was going to have to eat something to be polite.

The first thing he noticed as he entered the small front room were pictures of him and his sister all over the place. They were on the small fireplace mantle, they were on the piano, they were on the wall. He was a baby in some, a toddler in others. He was alone or sometimes holding his sister. His smiling face was looking back at him from under a baseball cap in one picture and an oversized cowboy hat in another. There were pictures he recognized and pictures he had never seen in his life.

He stopped in wonderment. His grandmother had continued into the kitchen. She returned to the living room to find out why he hadn't followed. She smiled with pleasure as he walked around the room looking at each picture, some large, some itsy-bitsy.

"Where in the world did you get all these?" He waved an arm around the room.

"From your mother."

"My mom? Did my dad know?"

His grandmother lowered her head in sadness. "I don't think so. He didn't write much."

Cameron thought that was an understatement if he'd ever heard one. After his dad had left for Canada to avoid getting drafted during the Vietnam War, he had severed all ties with his parents. His father had been a stubborn fool who wouldn't even acknowledge that he had a family. If asked directly, his dad would tell people that his parents were dead. It wasn't until his father had died that his mother had told him the truth. By then, his grandfather had been dead for years. Cameron had lived for so long without close relatives on either side that it was only a mild curiosity that he had a grandmother in the West. Yet he did find himself annoyed that his parents had kept this information secret. What else hadn't they told him?

"I never knew my mom kept in contact with you. Did you write her?"

His grandmother's face fell even deeper in despair. "No. For the first ten years after your father left, we didn't know what had happened to him. Then he met and married your mother in Canada. I only know this from your mother's letters. She started to write to us after you were born. That's when the pictures started to arrive. There was never a return address though. Over the years she kept writing and sending pictures. The postmarks changed pretty frequently. In the beginning they were from Alberta, Canada, then Michigan, then Kentucky."

"Wow. How strange. I knew I was born in Alberta, but I didn't know we lived in Michigan. I think of Kentucky as my home."

"Well, you lived in Kentucky the longest—since you were a toddler, I think—but even in Kentucky you seemed to move a lot."

"That's true. We did. Dad drove trucks and he was sort of restless, I guess. He was always changing companies looking for a better route. To be honest, he wasn't home much—most of the time it was just Caitlin, Mom, and me."

"That's what I gathered from your mother's letters. They were the only contact I had with your family." She smiled wistfully.

"There are pictures here I've never seen. I can tell you this, my mom certainly doesn't have pictures like this of me anywhere in the house."

The older woman smiled. "I wouldn't worry about that. I'm just a silly old woman. Now come sit down and have some enchilada casserole."

"That's Mexican food right?"

"Yes. Do you like Mexican food?"

"Don't know—never had it."

"What do you mean you've never had Mexican food? Ever?"

"Not really. It's not really popular in Kentucky. We're more of a meat and potatoes state—lots of barbecue too."

"Well, you're in California now, and Mexican food is a staple here. Come and try some. My visiting teachers brought it over just a while ago. You probably saw them leaving as you pulled up."

"The two women in the red Honda?"

"Yes. They both live around the corner."

"Well, I can try it. Is it spicy?"

"I suppose it might be to you at first, but give it a while and Mexican food will grow on you, I promise."

Cameron and his grandmother went into the kitchen. If it were possible, there were more pictures of Cameron and Caitlin in there, but there were also pictures of other children. Some vaguely resembled Cameron and his sister.

"Who are these other kids?" he asked.

"Oh, for the most part those are Karen and Mike's kids. Karen and Mike are the closest thing you would have to cousins living in Roseville."

"I don't have any cousins—at least I don't think I do." At this point Cameron didn't know whom he was related to.

"Well, technically that's true. You don't have any first cousins. Mike is actually one of your second cousins. His father and your grandfather were brothers. Your father is Mike's cousin, which makes Mike your second cousin, and his children are your third cousins. You'll meet them tomorrow. We're invited over for dinner after church. They can't wait to meet you."

He looked more closely at the pictures dotting the kitchen walls and magnetized to the refrigerator. "How old are Mike's kids?"

"Well, let's see—the youngest, Drew, is five, and the oldest, Stacy, is about your age—I think she turned twenty last month. Then there are five more in between that."

"Five more what?"

"Five other third cousins."

"Mike has *seven* kids?"

"Yes," his grandmother said absently. She was scooping a large portion of an orange and red, grainy looking casserole onto a dish. She put it in the microwave and turned to face him. The look on his face made her laugh out loud.

"Don't look so astonished. The Richards side of the family traditionally has large families. Only your grandfather and I were the exception. Well, I suppose that would include your dad and mom also."

"You mean I have even more relatives than this second cousin Mike?"

"Heavens yes. Some live pretty close—in the Sacramento area. Some are in southern California. Some are in Utah and one moved to Mesa, Arizona. Family reunions can be pretty overwhelming if you're not used to all the people."

Cameron tapped his fingers on the tabletop nervously. This was not at all what he expected. He had thought he was coming to help an old lady, who didn't have anyone else. Why was his mother so insistent that he come when she obviously knew about all this other family close by?

SUNDAY

ameron awoke with a start. Daylight was seeping in under white wooden shutters and splashing him on the face. He had a moment of confusion as he tried to place his surroundings. Ah, yes. He was at his grandmother's. Cameron found he had slept remarkably well in what his grandmother had told him was his father's old room.

There was nothing "old" about this room though. His grandmother had evidently gone to great pains to fix it up for him. A creamy blue color adorned the walls, the smell of paint still lingering. The queen size bedroom set was new, including a new mattress (he had checked under the bedding). He had never slept on a new mattress in his life, and this one wasn't cheap. The sheets and duvet cover were equally fresh and of a quality he wasn't used to. When he went to hang his button-down shirts—which came from one dusty, old duffel bag—in the closet, he found a feather comforter. It was still in its original packaging, on the top shelf of the glossy, white closet.

Next to his bed was a matching nightstand and at the foot of the bed, a chest of drawers. He had carefully placed his three pairs of clean boxers in the top drawer. His four colored T's went in the next drawer down. He had nothing to place in drawers three and four.

On the nightstand were a reading lamp, a clock radio, and a picture of his father, which had been placed there by his grandmother. Only two things on the nightstand officially belonged to him: the watch he had bought from Sears a week before he left Fargo and his CTR ring. The ring had fallen out of his pocket the night before as he was undressing for bed. It had rolled across the soft woolen throw rug next to his bed and onto the polished oak plank flooring. It tapped against the five-inch white baseboard and plopped on its side.

Cameron picked up the ring off the nightstand and held it between his fingers. He hated that Lauren had told him it was a "Mormon" ring. He hated that he couldn't wear it now. He vowed that in the next day or so he would take a little bit of his savings and get himself a new ring. Maybe one with a cool black stone in it or even a diamond. Yeah, that was it. He would get himself a diamond ring. No one would confuse him with being a Mormon again.

As he lay in bed this morning, he thought about Lauren. He put both hands behind his head and looked up at the gently rotating ceiling fan. She was cute, but what a bunch of crock she was peddling. He couldn't believe she was involved with these . . . now what did his pastor call Mormons . . . oh yeah, cultists. That was it. It was a cult religion. Like the "Moonies" and "Witnesses." All his life, in every church he had ever attended, the word was out that you stayed away from Mormons. They were sneaky folks who tried to brainwash you to their way of thinking. What had Lauren said about the Book of Mormon? Something about it being written by Indians in Egyptian hieroglyphics? What kind of nonsense was that? Cameron rolled his eyes and shook his head. She was just a silly girl, and he had more important things to think about, like why his mom had made such a big deal about his coming to California.

He had called his house in Kentucky last night, but no one had answered. His mother didn't have an answering machine. His mother used to have one, but his stepfather hadn't believed in them, so she got rid of it. His stepfather hadn't believed in televisions, either, but his mother refused to give that up. Evidently, there was only so much she was going to do for love. Maybe that was why they divorced so soon after they married.

He could hear his grandmother in the bathroom next to his room. There was only the one bathroom in the house. He hoped she was almost done because he needed to use the facilities—soon. She had said she would be gone this morning to church but that she would be back by twelve fifteen. She said to sleep in and take it easy. She had showed him where the cereal was. She had unopened boxes of Trix and Frosted Flakes. He somehow gathered that these were not her normal breakfast fare. This afternoon they were supposed to go to his second cousin Mike's house for lunch.

Before he even had a chance to get out of bed, he heard the bathroom door open and close. Then the front door opened and closed. She was gone. Well, fair enough, this would give him a few hours to get settled in. Who was he kidding? He had nothing to unpack, nothing to do, and nowhere to go.

He got up, padded around the house for a few minutes, and then returned to his room. He didn't want cereal; he wanted eggs. He grabbed his keys and headed for the door. His grandmother had given him a house key last night, so he locked up the house and hopped into his Jeep. Retracing his path from the night before, he soon found himself on Douglas Boulevard.

His car was pulled into Mel's Diner by an unseen magnet. He parked and walked in. A kid with dry skin and chapped lips was the host this morning. His neatly typed name was "Matthew."

"Would you like a booth or the counter?" Matthew queried.

"A booth would be fine, thanks." Cameron glanced around the restaurant. He tried to make believe he wasn't looking for Lauren, but truth be told, he checked every square inch of the restaurant and she was nowhere to be found.

When a pleasant, older looking woman came to take his order he casually asked where Lauren was. "She doesn't work Sundays," was the simple reply.

His eggs were bright white with a yoke winking up at him. The toast was a golden brown, and the fried potatoes melted in his mouth. He was glad he had come.

Someone had left a copy of the *Sacramento Bee* on the table next to his. He got up and retrieved it. He needed a job. The paper had a large classified section. Regardless of why his mother had wanted him to come to California, the fact was, he was here. He didn't want to go back to Kentucky. He hadn't really gotten along with his stepdad before the divorce, which is why he had moved to Fargo in the first place. In Fargo he found he liked being on his own, but he sure as heck didn't want to go back to North Dakota—too cold for him. He was never going to live through another northern plains winter, if he could help it. So, if he had to live somewhere, it may as well be here. Besides, he had never had a nicer bed, or bedroom, in his whole life—that was just something he wasn't going to be able to give up easily.

In the classifieds there was a Toyota dealership looking for a mechanic. He tore the notice out of the paper and left a small hole in the section. He quickly folded the paper back up and placed it on the table where it had come from. With his contraband want ad in his pocket, he paid for his meal and then drove home to wait for his grandmother.

Cameron heard the sound of a car door slamming outside the house. He looked up from the couch to see his grandmother walking up the steps. She held the handrail with one hand, and a large purse in the other. She ascended with more spring than he thought old ladies normally had. He made a mental note to ask her how old she was. He couldn't believe how much he didn't know about her.

She was smiling as she entered the room. "Hello, Cameron. Did you sleep well?"

"I don't know if I would use the word 'well' to describe how I slept."

A look of concern swept across his grandmother's face. "Oh, dear."

"No, no. I didn't mean that I didn't sleep well. I meant that I slept so wonderfully that 'well' was inadequate to describe how nice it was."

His grandmother breathed a sigh of relief. "Oh, I'm so glad. Mike picked out the bed especially for you."

"Really? Why would he do that?"

"Oh, I guess I didn't mention that he owns a furniture store. When I found out you would be able to come, I wanted to make sure you had a nice bed. The one that was in there before was your father's old one—and I do mean old. Mike and Karen helped me get the room all fixed up. Karen and the kids painted it. Karen's daughter Stacy picked out the linens, which was a good thing. If I had picked them out they probably would have been pink and a lot more frilly. Stacy works at a discount bedding store. Anyway, I think it all came together beautifully."

"Yes, it did. I am still confused though as to why you have gone to all this trouble for me."

The older woman was motionless for longer than Cameron was

comfortable. When she spoke, the words came out in small, choked sounds. "You are my only child's only son. I have waited a lifetime for you to come home."

Cameron didn't know what to say. His grandmother obviously had had years of knowing about him through his mother, but up until a year ago, he had never even known that she existed. "Gramma," he said, using the casual pronoun with tenderness, "it's all wonderful and I thank you. I am still getting used to the fact that I even have a grandmother. Please forgive me if I've said something that offended you in any way."

"You have not offended me in any way, Cameron. I cannot imagine that you could. Are you ready to go to Mike's?"

He certainly was dressed. He looked down at his black Dickies. They were the closest thing he had to dress pants. With a denim blue, open-collared shirt, he had done his best to dress up for the occasion of meeting his extended family. He was dressed. Was he "ready?" was a completely different story, but he answered his grandmother in the affirmative. "Yes, ma'am."

"Good. Karen, Mike's wife, said she would come and pick us up."

"Pick us up?"

"Oh, maybe you didn't know. I don't drive anymore. After the car broke, I never got around to fixing it. Then after a while I decided I was too old to drive anyway."

"I didn't know that you didn't drive, but then I never really thought about it. I do drive, however, so perhaps I can take us, that is if you can give me better directions than my mother can."

Cameron's grandmother hesitated for a moment and then spoke. "What do you drive?"

"I drive a Jeep. It's the one out front. I'm sure you saw it."

"The one without the windows and doors?"

"Well, yes, but I'll help you in, and if I am going to live here now, you are going to have to get used to me driving you around in it."

"Oh dear. What if it rains?" the older woman asked with genuine concern.

"I have the soft top and doors for that. At least you can try it. I did try the enchiladas last night, remember?"

"Well, I suppose I can try. Should I put on slacks?"

"It might be easier for you in the beginning, but my mother got used to it pretty quickly, and I used to run her up to church and the store all the time."

"Give me a moment to change then."

Cameron went outside to wipe the dirt and dust off the passenger seat. In Fargo he had installed a pull-down step on the passenger side for his one-time girlfriend. It had turned out to be a bad investment, the girlfriend that is. The step was another matter. He unlatched the step and was glad he had it now. It was just the thing his grandmother would need to get into his Jeep. Just as he finished locking it in place, his grandmother came out.

She tentatively looked at the height of the Jeep. Cameron had raised it six inches, which meant the passenger seat was now about three feet off the ground.

"Oh my," she said.

"It's no big deal. Give me your hand." He stretched out his own.

She took a step up and then lifted her foot over the ledge and sat on the seat with a triumphant grin.

"See, Gramma, it was a piece of cake." Cameron ran around to the other side and threw himself into the driver's seat. His grandmother had found the seat belt and was latched in. Cameron started the engine. The low, loud rumble of the Jeep startled the older woman.

"It's okay, Gramma, it's supposed to sound like that. That means it's running good."

His grandmother raised her voice a little. "That's fine, dear. Do you know how to get back to the freeway?"

"As a matter of fact, I do. I went to Mel's Diner for breakfast this morning, so I know right where it is."

"Oh, well, that's good then. We aren't actually getting on the freeway. We are just going to take Douglas Boulevard toward the lake."

"What lake?"

"Lake Folsom. Mike lives pretty close to it."

They passed Mel's Diner as they made their way across town. It was a pretty drive after they left the business district. There were a lot of really nice housing divisions on either side of the boulevard. After about seven miles, they turned left on Auburn-Folsom Road. This turned out to be a two-lane road winding up into the foothills. With a turn here and a turn there, they wound further into the dense forest of oaks. The farther they drove, the more peaceful it got. Mike lived in an older subdivision of custom homes. Cameron was more impressed by the Corvettes and BMW's in the driveways, though, than he was with the houses. His cousin Mike must make some serious money selling beds!

They stopped in front of a large, colonial looking home, complete with pillars. On the front porch were two children squished into one chair. The younger one was reading a book to the older one. There was an older Chevy truck, a small beat-up import, and a newer minivan in the driveway. Behind the truck he could see the outline of a boat under a cover. The kids looked up from what they were doing to watch the Jeep slow down and then pull into the driveway. When they realized that Clara was in the vehicle, they hopped up in unison and ran up the granite steps into the house. Soon a cascade of people came pouring out of the house: big people, little people, and people in between.

"Aunt Clara, Aunt Clara!" a small redheaded boy screamed as he ran toward the passenger side of the Jeep.

"Aunt Clara, I can't believe you're riding in a Jeep," a teenaged boy around sixteen years old chimed in as he came around behind his brother.

A tall, dark-haired man came over to Cameron's side of the Jeep. "So you must be Cameron. Well, you sure do look like a Richards."

"That's what my grandmother tells me."

"How was your trip from Kentucky?"

"I came from Fargo, North Dakota, actually, and it was pretty good. I lost a U-joint as I was coming into Roseville, but it was an easy fix."

A woman about his mother's age came up and stood next to Mike. She appeared to be pregnant. "Welcome to California. We're all so excited to meet you. We can hardly wait to hear about your trip here. It's just so great that you're staying with Aunt Clara. You're all she's talked about for the past month."

"Month?" Mike said. "She's been talking about you since you were born."

Cameron was not used to all this attention. His first instinct was to toss his grandmother out of the Jeep and head for the hills.

"Come in, come in," Mike said. He held out a hand for Cameron.

If Cameron thought he wasn't prepared for meeting Mike's family, he was even less prepared for what happened next. On Mike's right hand was a gold CTR ring.

"You're a Mormon?" Cameron coughed out the words in surprise.

"Yes. You didn't know that? The whole family is."

"Your family?" Cameron said as he glanced around at the children dotting the landscape.

"Yes, the extended family also."

"Gramma Clara?"

"Yes, Aunt Clara too. I'm surprised you didn't know that. Well, you've only been in town less than twenty-four hours, what am I talking about? Of course you don't know much about our family, and we don't know much about you. That's why you're here."

"You mean for lunch?" Cameron asked tentatively. For some reason he wanted a yes to this question.

"Certainly for lunch too, but no, I understood from Aunt Clara that your mom wanted you to meet your dad's side . . . of . . . the . . . family . . . " Mike's words slowed to a stop, and he looked at Cameron questioningly. "Why do *you* think you're here?"

"To help my grandmother recuperate from her broken wrist."

Mike laughed out loud. "Help Aunt Clara recuperate? That's a hoot. Aunt Clara has more help where she lives than anyone else I know. I should have so much help."

"So I gathered," Cameron said with a little annoyance.

"Is that what your mother told you?"

"Yes," Cameron said between clenched teeth.

"Well listen, let's just put that aside for a while. Come in for dinner and meet your family."

Cameron sighed and decided Mike was right. Even if his mother had somehow tricked him into coming, he may as well meet these people he shared genes with. He hopped out of the Jeep and followed Mike up the steps.

The inside of the house was big. That was the only way he could describe it—*big*. Well, he guessed he could also use *large, huge, gigantic,* and *immense*. It had towering ceilings. Chalk white columns held up a catwalk that connected two upstairs portions of the house. Under the catwalk he could see into a tastefully decorated family room. The fireplace was the largest he had ever seen. It was like one you would see in a hunting lodge—a stone face that towered at least twenty-five feet high. He had never been in a house like this before—not in Kentucky, and certainly not in Fargo. He just hadn't ever run in crowds that had money. *Oh my gosh,* he thought, *I'm related to these people.*

Prior to lunch the whole family gathered in the dining room for a prayer over the food. His grandmother offered it. It was a surprisingly Christian prayer. The prayer even ended "in the name of Jesus Christ."

The adults, which included Cameron and his third cousin Stacy, sat in the formal dining room and used fine china—another first for Cameron. Six other kids sat around a long trestle table in the kitchen.

Dinner was unbelievable. There was tender roast beef, soft whipped potatoes, creamy lumpless gravy, deep green broccoli, and a tossed iceberg lettuce salad with the best Ranch dressing he had ever tasted. To top it off, they had made a cake that said "Welcome to CA, Cameron."

The subject of religion didn't really come up at dinner. It wasn't that anyone was avoiding it, but no one was making a big deal about it, either. He did notice that the older kids had CTR rings of one kind or another. Because Stacy was at his table, he noticed hers in detail. It was a small silver ring, with a glittery red background that made the CTR stand out.

They discussed how each other was related. It was finally decided that although Cameron was officially either a second or third cousin, it would make things easier if he just referred to his second cousins as Aunt Karen and Uncle Mike. That would make the rest of the family unofficially his first cousins. He could live with that.

As they were finishing up with dessert, Aunt Karen asked Stacy if she was going to the fireside that evening at the stake center. Cameron thought it was a little warm outside to be putting logs on anyone's fire—even if it was a steak house, but he kept quiet.

"Yes," Stacy replied.

"How are you getting there?"

"A bunch of us are going. I think Brianna is driving."

"Okay then, but don't stay out late. I have that ultrasound in the morning, and I need you to be awake when you're watching the kids tomorrow."

"No problem, Mom."

So she *was* pregnant. What would that make? Eight! He felt a tug on his pant legs. Drew, his five-year-old redheaded cousin, was anxious to get his attention.

"Do you want to see my Hot Wheels?"

Mike, Karen, Clara, and Stacy all started to shake their heads rapidly, in unison, as a signal to Cameron to tell the little boy no, but Cameron really did want to see Drew's cars.

"Sure. I love Hot Wheels. I have a big collection myself at my mom's house."

Drew's face lit up. Cameron turned to face those at the table. "I'll be fine."

"Well, don't say we didn't warn you," his Uncle Mike laughed.

At the top of the stairway, they turned left on the catwalk. It took them to a long hallway. They passed two doors on the right and one on the left. Up ahead were two more doors. Cameron figured it must be one more bedroom and a bathroom. The second door on the left led into Drew and Jared's room. Jared was the oldest son, Drew was the youngest. He didn't know how he was going to keep everyone straight. Drew pulled out a plastic bin from under his bed. He opened it to reveal cars, tracks, and connectors for the tracks.

"Hey, this is neat, Drew. What do you say we set up a course?"

"Okay," and Drew promptly dumped out the entire contents of his toy box in the middle of the dark green, carpeted floor.

Cameron heard the doorbell ring but didn't pay attention to it. He had kicked his shoes off and was sitting Indian style with Drew. They were concentrating on connecting the red and yellow tracks together. He could hear the soft laughter of girl's voices coming down the hall. His hair was falling in his eyes, so he lifted his head to push it back. At the same time he glanced up, the girls passed by the bedroom door.

Looking back at him out of startled green eyes was Lauren.

Cameron's mouth hung open and he didn't speak. He didn't know what to say. Lauren stopped dead in the hallway and two girls bumped into her from the back. Stacy looked from Lauren to Cameron and back.

"Cameron?" was all Lauren could manage.

"Lauren . . . hi . . . uh, what are you doing here?"

"I was going to ask you the same question. Hi, Drew." She smiled down at the redhead at Cameron's side.

"This is my family." He motioned his head around to include Drew and Stacy.

"Well, I'm confused, then, because I thought you said your family was from Tennessee or Kentucky or somewhere back east."

"Kentucky. And I did. My mom and sister are in Kentucky. I just found out today that this is my California family."

Stacy couldn't contain herself any longer. "Lauren, how in the world do you know Cameron?"

"Oh, we met at Mel's yesterday." Lauren motioned to the girl behind her. "Cameron, you remember Brianna?"

"Uh, hi." Cameron smiled at the waitress.

"Wait a minute." Lauren stopped, squinting her eyes as she tried to remember something important. "CTR. Your name is CTR. Cameron Thomas Richards. Richards! Oh my gosh, you even look like a Richards now that I think about it. Well, how weird is that?" Lauren shook her head from side to side in amusement.

"So how do you know my cousin Stacy? Do all Mormons know each other?"

The girls laughed in delight. Brianna answered for the group. "Not really, seeing as how there are over eleven million of us now. We just happen to know each other because we used to be in the same ward."

"Ward?"

Lauren looked at the other girls and spoke for Cameron. "He doesn't know very much about the Church . . . at least not the *authorized version*," she said with emphasis. To Cameron she said, "A ward is like . . . a congregation. It's just a name we use for designating certain geographical areas that we live in."

"Oh, like a parish in the Catholic Church?" Cameron asked.

"Exactly . . . well, not exactly. I think in the Catholic Church you can go to any parish you want. In our church they like you to stay within your ward. It is easier to take care of each other that way."

"Take care of each other?"

"Sure. Home teaching, visiting teaching, stuff like that."

"Except I don't know what the heck you're talking about."

Lauren let out a big sigh. "This whole thing must be pretty confusing to you right now."

"Yeah, kinda," Cameron said.

Lauren turned to Stacy. "Maybe we should take him to the fireside."

Stacy looked a little concerned. "Look, I don't have a problem with that, but based on what I am hearing from Cameron, he might."

"I give. What's a 'fireside'?" Cameron asked.

"It's a church meeting where a bunch of us gather to hear a speaker give an inspirational, or maybe motivational, talk. Tonight we're going to the stake house, but sometimes they're held at people's homes," Brianna said.

"Steak house? Like a restaurant?"

Again the girls tried to contain their laughter. Not that it was that funny, it was a common enough mistake, but this whole discussion was going nowhere fast.

Stacy spoke up. "Look, like I said before, I don't care if Cameron comes with us or not. He is more than welcome, but good grief, he only got here yesterday and from what I'm hearing, he doesn't even know what a Mormon is. Don't you think a young adult fireside is pushing it a bit?"

Lauren sighed and Cameron thought maybe there was more in her sigh than what met the ear. He could sense that Lauren wanted him to attend for some reason. He shook the feeling off. He never planned on going in the first place. He wouldn't be caught dead in a Mormon steak house no matter how many relatives he had in this church.

Cameron shrugged his shoulders. "Hey, thanks for inviting me and all, but I couldn't go anyway. I promised Drew we'd put this course together, and then I have to take my grandmother home."

Stacy smiled in relief and said to the girls, "There you go then. Now we're going to be late. I'll show you the pictures later." The girls turned and went back down the hall. He didn't hear the front door open, but he heard it close.

It was ten in the evening, Kentucky time, when Cathy Richards answered the phone. She picked it up on the second ring. "Hello."

"Mom. Hope you were still up. Just calling to let you know I got here okay." Cameron was sitting on a wooden step stool next to his grandmother's old wall phone. He twiddled with the long phone cord.

"That's good. Have any trouble?"

"Oh, a U-joint went out, but that's about it." He absently picked up a pizza flyer. That sounded good for lunch tomorrow. Who was he kidding? That sounded good now—at seven o'clock, California time, he was hungry again.

"Where'd the U-joint go out? Was it expensive? I know you don't have much money."

"Right as I was getting into Roseville and not expensive at all. Only ten bucks or so. It was more time consuming than anything else."

"That's good. How's your grandmother? Have you met any other relatives from your dad's side of the family?"

"Well, yes, and I actually wanted to talk to you about that. What's the idea of you telling me my grandmother was an invalid?"

His mother snorted slightly in indignation. "I never said she was an invalid. I said she needed your help."

"Like heck she needs my help. She has an ace bandage around her wrist and as far as energy goes, she runs circles around me."

His mom sighed. "Cameron, not all help comes in a physical form."

"What's that supposed to mean?"

"Your grandmother is lonely. She's had a hard life."

"Hard life? You've got to be kidding. Have you ever met this woman? She is surrounded by people who love her. She has more family than you can shake a stick at and all I am is one more potential relative to suck her energy."

"Is that what she says? Or is that you projecting?" Cathy asked, her voice softer.

"Don't try that psychobabble on me Mom. You know what I mean."

"Actually I don't. Why don't you tell me."

"Well, for starters, she almost has a shrine set up in her living room dedicated to Caitlin and me—or to the *me* she thinks I am. How am I supposed to live up to what you have been feeding her for twenty years? And before you say anything about why you never told me about all this secret picture sending, save it, we'll get to that later. The point is, I'm not the person she thinks I am. I think there's a great potential for hurting a nice old lady's feelings, never mind that she is my grandmother."

"So is it uncomfortable there?" his mother asked with concern.

"No! That's just it. It's too comfortable. Do you know what she did? She went out and bought a whole bedroom set for me. She decorated this whole room in her house—for me."

"Well, that sounds wonderful."

"It's *not* wonderful. It's . . . it's strange. I feel like I'm staying in a new Motel 6. I don't belong here. And to top it off, they're all Mormons—Mormons, for Pete's sake! Why didn't you mention the whole Mormon thing? You know we hate Mormons."

"What do you mean 'we' hate Mormons. What have I ever said to you that lead you to believe I hated Mormons, or anyone for that fact?"

"Well, granted, maybe not you personally, but every church we ever attended bad-mouthed them. You're the one who sent me to those churches, so I'm assuming you agree with their philosophies."

"Cameron, that seems like a stretch to me. Since when have you known me to agree with anyone else's philosophies? I consider myself a pretty independent person."

"Yeah? Then why did you let *your husband* disconnect the answering machine?" Cameron spit the words "your husband" out. Right from the beginning, he had never gotten along with his mother's choice for a second husband. His anger was still evident in his voice. He never called him by his name.

"What are you talking about?"

"You know. He hated that answering machine, and you got rid of it after you got married."

"I didn't get rid of it because of Gordon." His mother laughed. "The old machine broke, and I never got around to replacing it. After a while I got used to not having to sort through all the junk phone advertisements. It was that simple."

"Oh. Well, there are other things."

"I'm listening."

"Just . . . just . . . never mind," Cameron said in frustration. "But this I do want to know. Why am I here? What am I doing in California? Why did you make such a big deal about me coming?"

"Look, Cameron. I'm your mother. I love you, but I'm not perfect. It just seemed like a good idea. You kept telling me how unhappy you were in Fargo, and I knew you didn't want to come back to Kentucky. I thought California might be somewhere you could start fresh and make something of yourself."

Cameron snorted into the phone.

"Here's the deal," Cathy said. "You know that your dad didn't want contact with his family after he left for Canada right?"

"Yeah."

"I didn't necessarily agree. After I became pregnant with you, I started sending letters to your grandmother. I figured maybe your dad had issues with his parents, but it was just plain cruel to not let them know about you. I never included a return address because I didn't want to rock the boat with your dad. He was already having problems enough with alcohol, and, well, it just didn't seem like it would make things better if he knew what I was doing. On the other hand, I refused to punish your grandparents because of your dad's stubbornness."

"Does Caitlin know all about this?" he asked.

"You mean about sending your grandmother pictures? No. But not because I am trying to keep it a secret. I just didn't think it was a big deal. I certainly didn't know she had them all out and framed. It's kind of sweet actually."

"Are you planning on sending Caitlin out here too?"

"I've thought about it, yes."

"When?"

"Well, not this summer, but maybe next, when she's sixteen. Also, it depends on how it goes for you."

"Is Caitlin home?" There weren't many things he missed in Kentucky, but his baby sister was one of them. He had been five when Caitlin was born and because she was premature, and ever so fragile, he had experienced her from a far more protective stance than most brothers.

"No. She's spending the night at her friend's house," Cathy said.

"Will you have her call me tomorrow?"

"Of course," his mother replied.

Cameron was quiet long enough for his mother to comment. When he finally did speak, his voice was tentative and shaky. "Mom, why didn't you tell us about Gramma when Dad died?"

Now it was his mother's turn to let the miles of silence between them lengthen.

Cathy's voice was distant with embarrassment. "I don't know." More silence, but Cameron knew she was not done.

When she spoke again, each word was measured, metered, and wrapped with emotion. "I was dealing with your father's death, and I wasn't ready to deal with your grandmother's life. I wasn't ready to deal with telling you and Caitlin about her. I suppose I was . . . weak." Her voice faltered at the end.

Cameron said simply, "I understand." And he did.

Cameron changed the subject, but it was no less unpleasant. "Mom, when did Dad start drinking? In Canada?"

Cathy was quicker to answer because this she had answers for, after years of pondering the question herself. "No, way before then—back in Roseville actually. But back then it seemed everyone was drinking. There was drinking and drugs and 'free love.' What a scam that turned out to be! When I met your dad in the early seventies, he was on fire. He was someone who stood for something. That meant a lot to me. He opposed the war in Vietnam when it wasn't a popular thing to do, and he actually acted on his convictions. After a while though, as the years wore on, it became burdensome to be so politically active. We were together for about ten years in Canada before you were conceived. It was during that time that his drinking started to take its toll, but by then I was pregnant and despite his drinking, I loved him dearly. He was a good man really. I still admire how he stood his ground. As it turned out, the Vietnam War was an emotional disaster for everyone.

There were no winners anywhere. Not the guys who went and not the guys who stayed—certainly not the people who lived in Vietnam."

"So Dad never talked to his parents after he left for Canada?"

"Not to my knowledge. At least not before the divorce. I suppose he could have afterwards, but I doubt it. He was a proud man—even when he was wrong."

"Well, Gramma acts like I am the prodigal son—but I'm not. I'm not Dad and it creeps me out."

"Honey, you are the same age as your dad was when he left, and you are her only connection to your dad. She's old. She's waited so long to be a part of your life. Can't you at least try to stay a little while? Are you thinking of returning to North Dakota?"

"Heck no. I'm never going shovel another sidewalk of snow as long as I live." They both laughed and it took their conversation back to a plane of normality.

"Does your grandmother live in a nice area? What about your other relatives? I don't know much about them."

"Gramma lives in an older neighborhood. It's nice though. She seems to have good friends close by. The other relatives—whoa, boy. Turns out the other relatives are practically made of money. Uncle Mike . . ."

"Uncle? Your dad had a brother?" Cathy said in genuine surprise.

"No. Mike is actually a second cousin or something. We just decided it was easier to call him uncle. Anyway, Uncle Mike owns a furniture store. That's where my bedroom set came from. Did I tell you I even have a new mattress set? It's really comfortable. So anyway, Mike lives in a really nice area about ten miles from Gramma's house. They are all Mormons too. In fact, it seems like the whole area is infested with Mormons."

"That doesn't surprise me. Your dad was a Mormon."

Black, empty silence came from Cameron's end of the phone. In a moment all the emotional ground they had recently covered had been rent apart.

After a few moments, his mother spoke again. "Cameron? Are you still there?"

"And you were going to tell me this when?" He let the last word linger on his tongue. His voice was edgy and rising.

"What? That your dad was a Mormon? I don't know. I didn't think it was that big of a deal. He was raised Mormon. He left the Church years ago, before Canada."

"*It's a big deal to me, Mom!*" Cameron shouted into the phone.

"Cameron, calm down. Your grandmother's going to hear you."

He lowered his voice, but only a bit. "She's not here. She's out walking."

"Well, calm down anyway."

"No! I don't want to calm down." He was breathing hard. "I've got to get off now. I'll talk to you later." Cameron didn't wait for a reply. He slammed the receiver down on its cradle.

He didn't care that he had probably upset his mother. What about him? He grabbed his keys, scribbled a note to his grandmother, and locked up the house as he left.

At first he just drove around the neighborhood. Then he became a man on a mission. He wanted a smoke. No sooner did the thought enter his mind than he saw a mini-mart up ahead. He parked on the street in front and ran in to get a pack.

He was shocked to find cigarettes were over four bucks a pack in California. He had never paid over a buck fifty in North Dakota and Kentucky. At this point he had very little cash to his name, but when it came right down to it, he didn't care. He didn't imagine that he was going to take up smoking again, at least not at these prices. This was a temporary fix to a complicated problem.

He came out and rummaged through the glove box for some matches. He lit up. Cameron took a long, deep drag on the cigarette. He leaned up against his Jeep. He knew as well as the next guy that cigarettes would kill you in the long run, but for now he needed the nicotine to calm himself down.

He also needed a plan.

That was the problem with taking his mother's advice—it came with her version of a plan. In this case she had failed to share both the intended outcome of the plan and a few major details. What did she think was going to happen, that he was going to move to the "Golden State" and everything would fall into place like it does in the movies? Did she think that by just living with a devoted grandmother that he was going to fall in love with the sweet old woman and her extended family? Was he now supposed to just forget everything he had ever been told, taught, or heard preached about Mormons? This wasn't just one minister, in one church, who decried Mormons from the pulpit. Every church he had ever been to warned against the teachings of this particular sect.

And what did it mean that his father was one of *them?* Granted, his father had the good sense to leave the Church—but what about his other relatives? How was he supposed to deal with them?

Well, he wasn't going to be pushed into anything, by anybody! He threw the butt of his cigarette on the pavement and ground it out with vigor. He put the cigarettes in the glove box and slammed the door. He wasn't going to be bullied by his mother or his grandmother, for that matter, although he had to admit that she hadn't done much bullying so far. But she was a mother, and he was sure her suffocating love was coming.

He drove home a bit calmer. A plan was, in fact, beginning to form. *The difference between Mom and me,* Cameron thought, *is that I take action when action is needed. When things got rough at home, I left for Fargo. When things got rough between her and Dad, she just toughed it out until Dad finally was the one to walk—even though Dad was the one who was mostly to blame—him and his stupid drinking. Well, that was weak on Mom's part.*

She may have been content to let her husband rule her life, but he sure as heck wasn't going to let another person dictate a lifestyle for him—not his mother, grandmother, or any of his newfound relatives. He was going to stick up for what he believed. He hadn't even been here two days, and this whole Mormon thing was already getting out of control. Well, no more. He was going back to his own church—as soon as he found one. He was going to get active in the youth program. He was going to put money in the collection plate. He wasn't going to let this Mormon virus infect him anymore.

MONDAY

*C*ameron was awake before the alarm on his watch went off. He had slept well after he had finalized a few things in his head last night. His grandmother was "grandmotherly" when he had arrived home. She offered him some store-bought cookies and milk when he walked in. If she had noticed the smell of cigarettes, she didn't comment on it. They had watched TV for a while, and he went to bed at the same time as she did—early.

This morning's plan was to get up, apply for the job at Toyota, find a jewelry store, and drive around looking for a church to join. He thought that maybe he would find one of those really nice larger churches. He and his mom had been to plenty of smaller, traditional churches in Kentucky. While he hadn't really attended church in Fargo, he had seen ads for more up-to-date churches that seemed to cater to his age group. The marquees had listed multiple services on Sunday, with multiple themes. You could pick both a convenient time and style.

He breathed in deeply and realized he could smell bacon. He loved bacon. It's going to be a good day, he thought as he dressed for the day.

"Good morning, Cameron. Did you sleep well?"

"Perfectly, thank you. I still can't get over what a comfortable bed you guys bought."

"Well, I'm glad you like it. I made some bacon and eggs for breakfast. Hope that's okay."

"I love bacon."

"How would you like your eggs?"

"Over easy, please."

"So, what are your plans for the day?"

"Looking for a job mostly. I found an ad for a mechanic at Toyota. I am going to go see about that. Then I thought I would just drive around and look at Roseville—get a feel for the place. Do you have a mall or anything here?"

"Actually we do. It's new. It's up off of Harding Well, actually, you go up Harding, then Harding turns into Galleria Boulevard, and after you pass the mall it turns into Stanford Ranch. I think the name changes one more time in Rocklin, but the mall itself is on Galleria."

"What's up with all the street name changes around here? I could barely find your house the other day because of it."

"I don't know. It's been like that the whole time I've lived here. I guess I'm just used to it."

"Well, I'm going to have to get a map. Do you know, by any chance, where the Toyota dealership is?"

"It's in the Roseville Automall. The easiest way is to go back toward downtown, get on Vernon going east, Vernon changes to Atlantic, and then Atlantic changes to Eureka. After you cross the freeway, you go right on Sunrise. You can't miss it."

"Right . . . I am definitely getting a map this morning," Cameron said shaking his head. "Also . . . well . . ."

The hesitation in Cameron's voice caused Clara to turn his way. "Yes?"

"It's not going to be a problem for you if I go to a different church on Sunday, is it?"

Clara laughed and returned to the eggs. "Heaven's no. I didn't even know you went to church."

"Oh, I do . . . I do."

"Which one?"

"Well, I haven't exactly found it yet, but I will today I think."

"No, I meant which church?"

"Oh," Cameron remembered the conversation with Lauren. Mormons got all caught up in wanting to know "which denomination." They seemed to have a hard time with the concept of Christianity for Christianity's sake. "Probably just a basic one. I think I am going to go to one of the community churches. They have more choices in programs and times of service."

"Oh, I see." Clara said, nodding her head in agreement as if he were a four-year-old child.

Cameron thought she couldn't see at all. Well, that was her problem.

He had just put another mouthful of egg in his mouth when the phone rang. His grandmother answered it and then handed the sturdy black receiver to him.

"Hello?" he said after quickly swallowing. His voice wavered as the food went down and the air came up.

"Cameron, is that you?" Caitlin said, momentarily confused at his warbling tone.

"Yeah. Sorry. I just swallowed something fast. It's good to hear your voice."

"Me too. Mom said I could call. What time is it there?"

Cameron looked at his digital watch. "It's 7:23."

"Oh. It's almost 10:30 here. What's California like?"

"Ah, where I am it's sort of like the outskirts of Nashville. There are small houses and pretty fancy ones."

"Oh. Are there big houses and stuff, like mansions?"

"Yeah, in some places. We have this uncle—Dad's second cousin, actually—but anyway, he lives in the biggest house I've ever been in."

Caitlin squealed in delight. "I can't wait to come. Mom said I can see Gramma next year if I bring my grades up." Cameron knew that grades had nothing to do with it. His mom had been using that old line with Caitlin as long as there was a Caitlin. It was meaningless—what Caitlin wanted, Caitlin got—and Cameron didn't begrudge his little sister one moment of pleasure.

"Mom said you and her got in a fight."

"Yeah. Sort of. Did she tell you why?"

"No. Well, something about Dad, but not the specifics."

"Ask Mom what religion dad was."

"Dad wasn't any religion. He never went to church—you know that."

"Yeah, well, that's what I thought too. Just ask her. But I don't want to talk about that now. What's going on with you?" Cameron felt a bit of sick revenge in telling his sister to ask his mother about their Mormon father. It didn't make him feel any better, because revenge seldom does, but he wanted to inflict a little pain on his mother, the same way he felt she had done to him.

"Nothing. Same old, same old. Sleep in, get up and watch TV, hang out with friends, go to Bible Study on Wednesdays and church on Sundays."

"Ah, summer at fifteen. I remember it well." Cameron sighed.

"What are you doing?"

"Well, this morning I will be looking for a job and then a church," Cameron said. He noticed his grandmother look his way. She was at the sink washing up.

"Which one?" Caitlin replied.

Cameron sucked in a short breath in surprise. "Which one what? Which church?"

"Yeah. What's around there?"

"I don't know yet. I haven't started looking."

"Oh, well, I may be changing churches. I went with my friend to hers the other day and I really liked it. They have this youth minister who is really, really hot." Caitlin let the last word roll off her tongue breathlessly.

"You are picking out your church based on a *hot* youth minister?" Cameron harrumphed in an older, wiser brother manner.

"Sure. Why not? I may as well be happy going to church. What's the big deal—they all use the same book."

"Yeah, but somehow that sounds rather shallow," Cameron said, but he knew he wasn't going to win any arguments with his sister, so he changed the subject. "Is Mom there?"

"No, she's at work."

"Oh. Well, actually, little sister, I gotta go. I really am leaving pretty soon to go see about a job. Call me later?"

"Sure. Mom said not to stay on the phone long with you anyway. Good luck on finding a job and oh," Caitlin added as an afterthought, "I'll pray for you to find the right church." With that, she hung up.

After the dishes were done, his grandmother found a surprisingly recent map that showed much of Roseville and the surrounding area. She used a yellow highlighter to mark the automall and Galleria. She circled out one tricky intersection and sent him on his way.

Once Cameron found Vernon Street, it was easy to get to the automall. He was impressed with its size. It had about ten different car dealerships in it. The Toyota dealership was in the back.

The manager he spoke to was a nice enough guy, but Cameron could tell he wasn't impressed by his experience. The manager said they had another position available as a lot boy—driving the cars in, out, and around the lot—but that was not what Cameron was looking for, at least not on his first day of trying to find a job. He left a little discouraged. As he got to his Jeep, he noticed a young kid looking under his truck.

"Can I help you?" Cameron asked, with a little more annoyance in his voice than he felt.

Startled, the kid hit his head on the front bumper. "Oh, sorry. Is this your rig?"

"Yeah."

"Sweet."

"What?"

"Ah, sweet? Sweet, looks good, fine?"

"Oh." Cameron nodded his head. "Thanks."

"Who lifted it?"

"I did."

"Really? The welding too?"

"Uh-huh. Why?"

"Nothing. You did a great job, that's all."

"Thanks. Wish your boss thought so."

"What? Did you apply for a job or something?"

"Yeah. The guy was not impressed with my experience. I didn't have any certificates."

"Oh, that. Yeah, they're big on certificates here. You should try one of the smaller places. Have you been to Rocklin Rollers 4x4?"

"No. This is the first place I tried. There was an ad in the paper."

"Oh. My name is Greg, by the way." He stuck his hand out.

Cameron reached back. "Cameron."

"If you really did this, and I'm not saying I don't believe you, you might want to try them. I heard that one of their mechanics rolled his truck up on the Rubicon the other day. He broke his arm. I think they might be looking for someone. They're a pretty busy shop."

"I've heard of the Rubicon. Is it close?"

"Not too far, maybe about forty miles."

"Cool. So how do I get to this Rock and Rolling place?"

"It's Rocklin Rollers, like Rocklin."

Cameron just shook his head in confusion.

"Oh yeah, you're not from around here. I did notice the North Dakota plates. Rocklin is the next town up. Get back on Sunrise, go north. Turn right on Pleasant Grove and left on Taylor. Taylor turns into Pacific, and it'll be about a mile up on your right. If the street turns back into Taylor, you've gone too far."

Cameron pulled a pencil out of his pocket and scribbled down the directions before he forgot them. "You've been a big help. Thanks."

"No problem, man. You do much wheeling?"

"Well, not yet, but I plan to."

"Well, I'll probably see you around. I drive a lifted, white '90s 4Runner."

"Straight axle?"

"Yeah."

Cameron shook his head in approval. "Cool."

Greg's directions to Rocklin Rollers 4x4 were perfect. The shop was a newer stucco affair sandwiched between two shuttered Victorian homes. Their beauty was tarnished with age, and they had been abandoned long ago. A puffing locomotive pulling flatbeds of sweet smelling lumber stamped with Roseburg, Oregon, heaved by on the tracks across the street. He pulled into the parking lot and was dwarfed between a raised Bronco and a raised Ford 250. A lifted Honda CRV was across from him. Behind the chain link fence he could see raised trucks and cars in various stages of repair. He liked the place already. The lingering, fragrant smell of cut pine mingled with crankcase oil—a guy's kind of smell. He breathed in deeply and walked in the store.

"No. I'm pretty sure I'm not going with blocks. I want leaf springs." The black kid at the counter tapped his fingers on the glass for emphasis.

"Leaf springs? Man, don't you know . . . " The conversation between the two young men behind the red and white checkered counter came to a stop when they noticed Cameron.

"Can we help you?" the black kid asked. The name on his shirt read "Donny."

"Well, I'm not sure. I was told you might be looking for a mechanic or something."

"Yeah, we are. Who told you?" the other kid asked. Cameron noticed his name was Rock. Seemed like an odd name. Not Rocky—just Rock.

"A guy at the Toyota dealership—Greg, I think."

"White '90s 4Runner?"

Cameron nodded. "That's him. He said one of your mechanics got hurt. Said you might be looking. I'm sort of new in town, and I want to work with cars, not fast food."

"We hear you, man. That your Jeep out there?" Donny motioned his head in the direction of the parking lot.

"Yeah."

"Cool."

"Thanks."

"So what do you do? Like what's your experience?" Donny asked.

"A little bit of everything, but I've been into wheeling for a while, so I can do most anything on my own rig. I worked at a full-service gas station in Fargo, North Dakota, for a year. Before that, I worked part time at a local repair shop in Kentucky. Also, I took a bunch of auto classes in high school."

"Any welding?" Rock asked.

"Some. I did all the welding on my own truck. Before I left Fargo, the manager at the station was letting me do most of the spot jobs."

"Well," said Donny, shaking his head approvingly, "it sounds like you'd better talk to Roland. He's the owner." Donny turned and went out a side door, leaving him and Rock alone.

"Rock. That a nickname or something?" Cameron asked.

"Something like that."

"Short for Rocklin?"

"Oh, heck no." Rock let out a short, snorting laugh. "Short for 'rock of my salvation.'"

"Oh, really?" and Cameron let the words slowly roll off his tongue.

"Yeah. You been saved?"

"Funny you should ask. I was when I was a kid, and I am looking for a good church around here now. I'm living with my grandmother in Roseville and haven't really found a place to go yet. What do you recommend?"

Rock lowered his voice and leaned toward Cameron. "The bosses don't like me preaching or nothing, but seeing as how you asked me, I suggest The Arm of Christ. It's over on Riverdale Road. Near downtown. I go there myself. Pastor Jack is a real character, but he is solid with the spirit. We're meeting tonight as a matter of fact. If you have time, why don't you come on down?"

"I might. What time?"

"Five-ish. We're having a potluck, but you don't need to bring anything, just come."

At that moment the boss entered the shop. Cameron and Rock both straightened up and watched him come toward the counter.

Breathing heavily, Roland stuck out a beefy hand toward Cameron. Cameron shook it.

"So, I hear you're looking for a job. Donny tells me you've done some welding in the past." Roland grinned at Cameron. He was a big guy. He filled out his blue XXXL coveralls. In fact, the buttons were almost vertical with the strain of keeping his grease-stained uniform together.

"Yeah, in Fargo. Toward the end, I was doing most of it at the station. I did my own rig too, when I lifted it."

"Well, tell you what. I own this shop and so I get to do the hiring. I really need a guy who can weld—so let's take a look at your Jeep. If I like what I see, you're hired. That's the fun of being your own boss." Roland winked at the other two employees as he headed for the door with Cameron.

An hour later Cameron was on his way, employed. He had gotten a much better job than he expected. Tomorrow he would be working full time—Monday through Friday—weekends off. In thirty days he would get medical and dental benefits if he worked out.

He was feeling good about life, and to top it off, tonight he would go to The Arm of Christ Church with Rock.

As he drove toward the mall in Roseville, he uttered a short prayer of thanksgiving. "Father who art in Heaven, thank you for this job.

Thank you for introducing me to Rock. Help me to find the truth. In Jesus' name, amen."

The mall was a mall. It had the requisite Sears and JC Penney—one store to buy your tools and the other to buy your clothes. He parked close to Sears and as luck would have it, entered through the tool department.

The Sears-red of the Craftsman tool chests drew him deeper into the department. He pulled the drawers out of the mechanics' chest. The quiet, gentle glide of the drawers was sweet music. He lifted the largest wrench he had ever seen—two feet of torque that could tighten the bolts on a space shuttle. He sat on riding lawn mowers and dreamed of getting a charge card with his name on it.

In his daydream his four-car garage was filled with shiny red tool chests and an engine hoist. He could feel the cool black handle of a three-ton jack. No, his garage would have a professional lift. Yeah . . . He closed his eyes so he could picture his garage in more detail.

Outside his dream garage, he could hear the voice of Lauren.

His eyes popped open. Lauren? Who invited her into his dream? Then he realized he actually could hear Lauren's voice, close by.

He turned to see her arm in arm with a tall, golden-haired boy. They were walking toward the exit. She was saying something about not liking the suit he had just picked out.

He took a step back in the aisle to avoid being seen. So Lauren had a boyfriend. Well, that was okay. He was through with this "pretty Mormon girl" anyway. Tonight he would probably meet up with some girl from The Arm of Christ. She would have dark hair and a nice tan. She would be a great cook and like four-wheeling. He wasn't worried. Maybe tonight he would meet the girl of his dreams, not the girl in his dreams.

Seeing Lauren again made him realize why he was at the mall in the first place—to replace his CTR ring.

He entered the mall proper and started looking for a jewelry store. As luck would have it, the first jewelry store was next to Sears. The store was empty of customers.

"May I help you?" an older gentleman in a black suit asked.

"Maybe. I am looking for a nice men's ring," Cameron replied.

"Rings, we have." The clerk motioned to a display case. Silver and gold rings adorned a black velvet background. "What did you have in mind?"

"Something simple and cheap, actually. I am looking to replace a ring." Cameron lifted his hand to show the white band of flesh where his CTR ring used to be.

"Oh, I see. Lose it?"

"Well, I guess you could say that," Cameron said.

"Silver or gold?"

"Silver. I doubt if I can afford gold."

The clerk unlocked the case and pulled out two rings: a slender band with a flat, black stone imbedded in it, and a plain silver band.

Before Cameron tried them on, he picked up each one and looked at the price tags. The first ring was $329 the second was $189.

"Ouch," Cameron said.

"But do you like either one? Don't worry about the price right now. We can work something out," the clerk offered.

"I like the more expensive one of course."

"Of course." The clerk smiled. "I can take 35 percent off. We're having a big sale this weekend, and I could just give you the sale price a little early."

"Well, to be honest, even your sale price is a little high for my budget."

"What's your budget?"

"Under $75, actually."

The clerk rolled his eyes slightly. "Well, have you tried Sears or JC Penney? They might have something more in line with your budget." At that moment a woman entered the store and without a word, the clerk walked her way, leaving Cameron alone by the display case.

"Nice talking to you too, buddy," Cameron said under his breath as he walked out of the store.

Back in the belly of the mall, Cameron weaved in and out of the kiosks. He was impressed by the weirdness of the products being peddled. He found he liked a "rolly" thing that went up and down your spine and looked like an alligator. A short, Asian booth-girl had demonstrated it on his back, but there wasn't really anyone at home whom he wanted to rub his back, so it was easy to walk away.

A store he had never heard of caught his eye: Pineapple Democracy.

He liked the window display of men's khaki pants, plain-colored T-shirts, and plaid shirts enough to enter the store.

"May I help you, sir?" an exceptionally cute, bouncy, blond teenager asked him. Her hair swayed slightly as she walked toward him. She was dressed in the female version of the male mannequin: khaki pants, tight tan and white striped tank top with an open, white, button-down shirt over it. She had a soft lisp from her retainer and a hint of blue sparkle stuff on her eyelids.

"Sure, I guess. I am looking for some khaki pants like the ones on the display guy out front."

"I'll be happy to get them for you. What size do you need?" The employee had on a tag, but it only said "Pineapple Democracy." Cameron thought that was a bit weird. Why even bother with a nametag if you're not going to give your name? He wondered if it was to keep guys from hitting on the cute female employees.

"Thirty waist, thirty-four long," Cameron said.

"Would you like me to pick you out a button-down to match?"

"No . . . ah, well, sure. Why not? I'm going to a church thing tonight, and I didn't really want to go in jeans and a T-shirt."

"What church?"

Cameron jumped slightly. "What?"

"Oh, I'm sorry. I didn't mean to startle you. I just wondered what church you were going to?"

Cameron glanced down at her hands. She had on a ring, but it was just a dolphin or a porpoise—he couldn't tell which. It didn't look like a CTR ring to him. "I'm going to The Arm of Christ in Roseville."

"Oh. Well, that sounds like fun. Hey, I'll go get your clothes and meet you at the fitting rooms." She motioned with her head to an archway at the opposite side of the store.

"Okay," Cameron said as she walked off. She seemed like a nice enough girl, sort of like a young Lauren. Dang it, he did not want to think about Lauren. When he got to church tonight, he was going to steer clear of blondes. Seventy-four dollars lighter, Cameron left the "pineapple stand." He had one pair of pants and two sale shirts. He threw them into the back of the Jeep and headed for home, or at least to his grandmother's, to change before the dinner meeting at what he hoped would be his new church.

The first thing Cameron noticed as he pulled up to The Arm of Christ Church was that it was in a strip mall, an old, run-down strip mall at that. Not that God's church couldn't be found in many types of locations, he was just expecting something a bit more traditional. The parking lot was full. The cars probably said a lot about the congregation—young and struggling. Well, that could be a good thing. Humble folks were probably more welcoming and less critical of newcomers.

He parked next to a blue, '85 Honda. It had one red passenger door and a cracked windshield. Maybe he was being guided to this place because they needed a good mechanic—but wait, Rock was here. Maybe what he needed to do was to stop trying to analyze the situation and just go in.

The plate glass windows had vertical blinds keeping the afternoon sun out. He walked up to the door and let himself in. The first thing that assaulted him was loud Christian rap music coming from some tinny speakers. The second thing that caught him off guard was the crowd. They were young, all right; there didn't appear to be one person over twenty-five, with most of them just teenagers. There were about five little kids running around and two or three babies in car seats or strollers.

The crowd was predominately Mexican. A few of them stopped talking for a moment and turned to stare at him as he stood fixed to the chipped linoleum floor of the old retail shop. Toward the back of the room, he caught the eye of Rock, who smiled and rushed over to meet him.

"Hey, Cameron. I didn't know if you would actually come. Come on in and let me introduce you to a few of my brothers." Cameron took this to mean his brothers in Christ, because Rock clearly was not Mexican and these guys were clearly not his real brothers. Rock was a slightly built, wiry, little, white fellow.

"Alfonso, this is Cameron. He's starting work tomorrow at the shop."

"Hey, man." Alfonso nodded his head and held out a tattooed arm. "Jesus loves you, man."

Cameron nodded and smiled back. He could feel the stares of some of the other people in the room. He was feeling awkward and overdressed; most of the people were in loose, black pants and tight, white T-shirts—including the girls. Before he could say anything to Alfonso, the door opened again. This time a young girl with a bright pink Mohawk walked in. Her hair was shaved short on the sides of her head and stuck straight up five inches on the top.

"Belinda!" Rock laughed and motioned for her to come over. "I want you to meet a new friend of mine."

Belinda walked over. She smiled at Cameron. She had one prominent gold tooth, a pierced tongue, a nose ring, an eyebrow stud, and more than ten gold earrings, and what appeared to be some sort of horn sticking through one of her ear lobes. Cameron tried not to stare.

"Belinda, Cameron. Cameron, Belinda."

"Nice to meet you, Cameron." Belinda had a slight lisp from the pierced tongue.

"Likewise." Cameron didn't know what else to say.

"Come on, man, come have some dinner," Rock said. He started walking toward the back of the church. The whole group gathered around a folding table filled with potluck dishes. Rock offered the prayer. He looked up toward the peeling paint on the ceiling panels and raised his arms.

"Jesus, great Jesus. Bless this food. Bless this congregation. Bless this world with peace. Jesus, thanks for the blessings of the spirit you pour out on us daily. Amen."

The group gave a communal "Amen, Jesus."

He wasn't surprised to see there was a whole Mexican feast laid out. He didn't know what the food was, but he was pretty sure he wasn't going to try it. The enchilada casserole the other night was pretty adventurous for him. Over on a hot plate were some hotdogs that had, at one point, been boiled until they had split open on the sides. Now they were lukewarm, with a faint oily covering on top of the water.

"Actually, Rock, I'm not that hungry, I had a big lunch. In fact, I can't even stay too long," Cameron lied. "I told my grandmother I would go with her to my uncle's tonight. She doesn't drive." Well, part of that was true. His grandmother was going to his Uncle Mike's and she didn't drive. Of course, he had told her when he got home from the mall that he wasn't going to be able to go to Mike's at all because he was going to his new church. Now that he was here, he could see that this wasn't the place for him. If he turned around and went back to his grandmother's right now, he could drive her over. He was pretty sure the food at Uncle Mike's was going to be better than this.

"No problem. Services on Sunday are at ten."

"Great, maybe I'll see you there." *Was it a sin to lie in a church?* Cameron thought.

As Cameron drove back toward his grandmother's, his thoughts turned toward a pastor he had particularly liked in Kentucky. He had shared in a Sunday sermon something that Cameron had never forgotten. It had struck him as so true that he was ever after surprised that more Christians didn't adhere to it. It was a simple enough thing: Pastor Fredrick had shared the way all Christians should pray.

Prayers, he had said, were to be modeled after the Lord's Prayer in the New Testament. They were sacred and should be treated as such. In fact, it was called the Lord's Prayer because our Lord taught it to his disciples. Pastor Fredrick said it was found in both Matthew and Luke, proving how important it was. Matthew included it in the Sermon on the Mount and Luke included it as an answer to a request from one of his disciples. There were some small differences in the form in which the two disciples recorded the prayer, but Pastor Fredrick said this could be accounted for by supposing that the disciples themselves did not always use exactly the same words in saying the prayer. Pastor Fredrick said that when Christ uttered his famous prayer that it was as much about teaching us how to pray as it was an actual petition to his Father.

Now, all of Cameron's prayers followed the same basic format. He always petitioned his Father in Heaven, thanked him for his blessings, and asked for his help, in Jesus' name. His prayers were sincere petitions for help from his Father in Heaven. He liked to pray. He liked the calm feelings it brought to him. He sometimes prayed on his knees before he went to bed, but he was more likely to pray while he drove.

He did so now. "Father in Heaven, thank you for the blessings of having a mind that I can use to make decisions with. Thank you for my mother, who tries her best to make my life more workable. Thank you for my grandmother, who really seems to love me, even though she's just met me. Heavenly Father, help me be a son and grandson that they can be proud of. Help me . . . " He had to stop midsentence to brake for a cat crossing the road.

"Help me to find the right Christian church to attend. Lead me by thy hand to the one you want me to attend. Help me to get along with my new Mormon relatives, maybe even help me to understand them a bit. In Jesus' name, Amen."

Cameron had no sooner finished his prayer than he found himself on his grandmother's street. He sighed. It felt right to pull in the driveway.

His grandmother wasn't home when he got there. He decided he could find his Uncle Mike's house okay on his own, so he headed back into town. He found himself looking into the Mel's parking lot as he passed it, but for what he didn't know. It wasn't like he knew what car Lauren drove. In fact, he didn't know for sure if she even drove—her mother had picked her up that first night. The parking lot was full, which meant the restaurant was full, which meant they probably had a full crew on, which meant Lauren was probably working.

Cameron shook his head vigorously and clenched the steering wheel with his fingers. Why couldn't he get this girl out of his mind? She was trouble for sure. She was a Mormon, and not just a casual one. She honestly seemed to believe the malarkey this cult was peddling.

Once again Cameron felt his thoughts turn heavenward. He whispered over the sound of Shania Twain on the radio, "Dear Father, thank you for my grandmother's hospitality, but help me to find the real truth. Help me to find your truth. Help me to find the church you want me to attend while I am here in California."

He took a deep breath and felt much calmer. Prayers were like that, they really did help to stop the frayed edges of his life. He could now take in the oak-studded views that surrounded him on his way to Mike's.

He pulled in the driveway and shut off the motor. As the jeep quieted down, he could hear singing coming from the backyard. Then it became quiet for a moment, and then he could hear the sounds of his cousins shouting and jumping in the pool.

He considered ringing the doorbell, but clearly the family was in the backyard, so he just let himself in the side gate. As he rounded the corner, he stopped short for a moment. His Uncle Mike was standing behind his Aunt Karen. Mike was in his bathing suit, his tan frame solidly behind his wife. His hands were gently resting on Karen's bare shoulders, her tummy showing the full extent of her pregnancy. The back of Karen's head rested on Mike's chest. The closeness they shared was obvious. He had never seen his parents in such an intimate pose, yet what was so intimate about a husband's hands resting on his pregnant wife's shoulders? From his position behind the corner of the house, he could actually feel the love that his uncle and aunt shared. How weird was that? He felt a bit embarrassed that he was witnessing such a tender moment. But then this tender moment was happening in front of all the children, who were paying no attention to it, and in front of his grandmother, who was equally unaware of the intimacy of the moment going on. He apparently was the only one who saw the special bond between Mike and Karen. Before he stepped from behind the corner of the house, Drew saw him.

"Cameron! You came! Aunt Clara said you were at church—but I knew you weren't because nobody goes to church on family night." The red curls on the top of his head bobbed as he shook his head and rolled his eyes at the very thought of this concept.

Now everyone was looking his way, smiles all around, especially his grandmother.

"Well, Drew," Cameron said as he came out of the shadows, "I actually did go to church, but . . . " *But what*, he thought. "But it turned out to be the wrong church for me." Cameron noticed out of the corner of his eye that Mike winked at his grandmother. What was that about?

Mike came over and put his arm around Cameron. "Come join us. We were just getting ready to put the steaks on. You're staying for dinner aren't you?" He didn't wait for Cameron to answer. "Of course you are. You would be out of your mind to miss one of my steak dinners."

"Of course I'm staying for steak," Cameron replied.

"Are you coming to our family night too?" Drew innocently asked.

Cameron bent at the knees in order to look Drew in the eyes. "I don't know. What's family night?" Cameron could feel the anxious eyes of his extended family on him. He looked around the group with a questioning glance. "What?"

"Family night. You know, dummy."

"Drew!" Aunt Karen raised her voice slightly. "You know better than to speak to Cameron that way."

Drew lowered his eyes.

Cameron put his hands on his young cousin's shoulders. "I really don't know what family night is. Why don't you tell me."

"Well . . . we sing a song, then we pray, then someone gives a lesson, then we have food—like a dessert or something." Drew looked to his parents for confirmation that he had gotten it right. They were nodding and smiling at Drew.

"Hum . . . so is that why I heard you all singing back here?"

"Uh-huh."

"So who gives the lesson?"

"Everyone."

"Everyone gives a lesson?" Cameron's eyebrows pulled together. This was going to be a long night.

Drew giggled. "No, silly, not everyone at the same time. We take turns."

Mike interceded, "Tonight Stacy is giving the lesson. They're pretty short. It's not like a sermon at church." He turned to Stacy. "What is the lesson on tonight?"

"Baptism," was Stacy's reply.

"Oh, I didn't know Mormons believed in baptism."

"We do. Very much so. Family home evening is sort of a special time for our family, and now that you're a part of that, we'd love for you to stay," Mike said.

"Well, sure. I can stay. I don't have a hot date, that's for sure."

"Can you go swimming with me?" Drew had wiggled from under Cameron's hands and was racing toward the pool.

"I didn't bring my suit. I think I'll just sit here with Gramma Clara for now." He crossed over to an empty seat next to his grandmother.

"I didn't expect to see you. How was the meeting at your new church?"

Cameron hesitated to tell his grandmother that this church had not been all he had thought it was going to be—that in fact, it had been sort of a depressing event for him. He wanted to be in control over his own religious choices but hadn't really found what he was looking for yet.

"Truthfully, it wasn't what I thought it would be."

"How so?" Clara took a sip of her lemonade and put it on the glass top of the patio table.

"Well, for starters it was in a strip mall. Not that God can't be found in strip malls, but I was looking for a more traditional type of church."

"Little white building with a cross on top and stairs leading to wide double doors?"

Cameron looked at his grandmother sheepishly. "I suppose."

"I went to a Baptist church like that when I was younger."

"Really? I thought you were always a Mormon."

"Oh no, I converted after I met your grandfather. He actually baptized me. I met him while he was on his mission in Mississippi. I was the only one in my family who converted, though. The rest of my family was pretty much against me joining. It got a little ugly, actually. Anyway, the whole time my family was having trouble with my baptism, I had been writing to your grandfather, after he had gone home, of course. One day he invited me to come visit with his family. I did, and the rest is history."

"So you were a Baptist before you were a Mormon?"

"Yes."

"That's kind of spooky. I went to Baptist churches too. Didn't the pastors . . ." Cameron lowered his voice and leaned toward his grandmother, "warn you about the Mormons?"

Clara burst out laughing. "Oh yes, they warned me. They warned my family. They were pretty adamant that I was going straight to H-E-double toothpicks."

Cameron smiled at his grandmother's avoidance of the word *hell*. All his life he had been taught about hellfire and damnation—and being baptized a Mormon was a surefire, one-way trip to Hades.

"So you joined the Church because you fell in love with Grandpa?"

"No. I joined the Church because I fell in love with the gospel of Jesus Christ."

"But you had the gospel of Jesus Christ as a Baptist."

"True, I learned of Christ in the Baptist church. I knew the Bible stories by heart. I studied the New Testament, but I didn't fully know Christ until I joined the Church, The Church of Jesus Christ of Latter-day Saints."

Cameron leaned back on two legs of the wrought iron chair with a perplexed look on his face. "I don't know. I've just heard too many weird things about Mormons. They have the 'Golden Bible' and then what about all those wives? But for me, I think the biggest deterrent is that they seem to believe they can earn a place in heaven by just doing good works. They don't believe in the grace of God."

Clara patted Cameron's hand and sighed. "I know, I know. I was once where you are now."

"Well, to be honest, I just can't buy it, and obviously neither could my dad." Cameron let the tipped chair fall to the ground. He was getting agitated. He thought vaguely about the cigarettes in the glove box of his Jeep.

"That's not a condition for you living with me. That you 'buy it.' This isn't about you and the Mormon Church. This is about you as a member of a larger family. You know that, Cameron, don't you?" Clara said with genuine concern in her voice.

"I know. I'm not saying you are pushing this Mormon thing on me. I just feel so much conflict about finding out that all my relatives, the ones I didn't even know I had, are Mormon."

"We're your family first, Cameron," Clara said softly.

"I know." Cameron lowered his head in slight embarrassment. "I don't mean to seem ungrateful."

"You don't. This is all new. You just need time to adjust. Once you get to know your father's side of the family, I am sure you will grow to love them."

Cameron glanced around the backyard. The scene was almost pastoral: his younger cousins were still in the pool, his aunt was setting the wooden table near the pool, and his uncle was tending the barbecue. The smell of Black Angus beef broiling made him involuntarily lick his lips. Stacy was curled up on a lawn chair reading what appeared to be scriptures. A phone was ringing in the house.

"Gramma, loving them is not the hard part—but fitting in may be."

The phone stopped ringing and then started up again. No one went to answer it. Cameron glanced around to see if anyone but him was hearing the phone. The phone stopped. When it began to ring for the third time, Mike exchanged worried looks with Karen and ran to get the phone. He must have just missed it because a moment later it started ringing again. This time the whole family had taken notice and started to gravitate toward the house to see who was calling. One by one the family tentatively entered the kitchen nook behind their parents. Stacy pulled a chair up near where her dad was talking.

"Okay . . . okay . . . you need to calm down if you can," Mike was saying to the person on the other end of the phone. "Can you explain where you are?"

Karen positioned herself next to Mike and raised both hands in a questioning gesture.

Mike gestured back. He mimed writing on the palm of his hand.

Karen pulled a pad and pencil out of a nearby drawer.

"Lomida trails? Up near the equestrian staging grounds? Oh, past them. You mean on the horse trails? Wait, calm down for a bit . . . Are you saying that when I get to the end of the road, I need to drive on the horse trail?" Mike tapped his pencil as he listened. "Uh-huh . . . okay . . . but I'll have to call Brother Powers first. He has an F 250 4x4. It will probably take twenty minutes or so. Okay . . . no . . . look, you need to catch your breath and I'll be right there. I'll take my cell phone, but I get lousy reception near the lake so just know I'm on my way and everybody here will be praying for you guys." Mike motioned for Karen to get something out of the refrigerator. She quickly located a small glass vial of what looked like cooking oil and handed it to Mike.

"Brianna, you've got to pull yourself together and let me get off the phone." Mike motioned for Stacy to come to him. "Listen, you can stay on the phone to Stacy while I'm on my way."

Mike handed the phone to a startled Stacy and then turned to Karen. "Some of the young adults were out four-wheeling and rolled Zachary's truck."

"The Toyota?" Jared asked.

"I don't know. I guess. I think maybe one of the girls is hurt but I can't get Brianna calmed down enough to figure it out. Can you go get the first aid kit out of the boat, and I'll run and get out of this bathing suit."

"Uncle Mike?" Cameron spoke for the first time.

"Yes?" Mike paused.

"I have my Jeep. It can go anywhere, and I already have a first aid kit with me. Why don't I drive you?"

"Perfect." Mike motioned to his oldest son. "Jared, go and take care of the steaks and save a couple for Cameron and me." As Mike started for the stairs, he grabbed his cell phone and started dialing.

Ninety seconds later Mike was coming down the stairs two at a time. He was giving directions on the cell phone to someone. He had changed into jeans and a Cougars T-shirt. He motioned with his head for Cameron to follow him.

Cameron was right behind him as they passed through the garage to the front of the house. Mike stopped and picked up some rope and miscellaneous tools. Cameron shot ahead of him and jumped into the Jeep. Mike was right behind him. They both put on their seat belts, and the Jeep kicked up some gravel as they backed out the driveway. Mike motioned for him to turn left, back toward Auburn-Folsom Road. He was on the phone again.

"Terry, this is Mike, listen. A couple of kids from the ward just had a rollover accident up near the lake. Yeah, I'm on my way. They're on some horse trail or something. My nephew Cameron is driving me there now in his Jeep. Yeah, that's what I thought too. Right, from Kentucky. I know . . . Okay, so you know where to meet us. Perfect."

It was always weird when people talked about you, with you right there next to them.

Mike hit the "end" button on his phone and spoke to Cameron. "Sorry, for dragging you into this. I don't actually know what happened. All I could get from Brianna is that a kid in our ward, Zach, rolled his truck and there were three kids in it at the time. Brianna thought two of the kids didn't have their seat belts on. She ran up the hill to get reception on her cell phone, so she wasn't sure who was hurt or how badly. She sounded pretty upset. Oh, you need to turn at the next right."

Cameron slowed to make the turn. He kept going up a hill, but the street was much narrower.

"We are going to have to go on some kind of a horse trail. I am not sure how wide the trail is. Brianna said it winds down toward the lake and that we need to keep going on the trails to the right. They rolled it on a trail right before you get to the water."

The end of the street opened up to a broad cul-de-sac. On one side was a large parking lot with a brown government sign announcing it as the Equestrian Staging Grounds. On the other side of the cul-de-sac was a baseball field with a Little League game in progress. There was a slender opening between the trees that marked the start of the horse trails. The trail on the left was flat. The one on the right continued to climb into the oak-studded forest. They took the trail on the right. Cameron pulled the lever next to the manual stick to engage his four-wheel drive. The front hubs locked. The Jeep shimmied as it moved up the rocky trail. Mike reached up and grabbed the roll bar for support. The air was cooler and the light was dappled under the canopy of trees. This kind of wheeling was what Cameron lived for. Smaller trails crisscrossed the main trail. They reached what appeared to be the summit and began their descent. Cameron pulled the manual stick into four-low. He let the Jeep crawl down the hill in first gear. The ground was dry, and his knobby tires kicked up the soft, parched dust of the trail. It left a choking haze around them that made him and Mike cough. Occasionally they could see snippets of the blue lake below. They came to a hairpin turn with a fence on one side and a large boulder on the other.

Mike spoke. "I really appreciate your doing this, Cameron. I can see now that it takes a pretty special kind of truck and driver to get out on these trails. Man, am I glad you decided to come over for dinner." They hit a particularly deep rut in the trail, and the Jeep jerked to the side. Mike's free arm waved in the air as he tried to balance himself against the gyrating of the vehicle in motion.

Cameron turned right at the bottom of the trail. He and Mike could see the Toyota truck in the distance. Mike let out a small moan, but Cameron didn't think it looked that bad. It was just tipped over on its side—happens all the time to guys four-wheeling. Of course, it was pretty stupid if the kids riding with him didn't have their seat belts on. This Zach kid was obviously not a serious "wheeler" because you *never* let anyone in your rig who doesn't buckle up. If you get in an accident, like Zach had done, and people get hurt, you could end up losing not only your rig but also your license! He knew plenty of kids in Kentucky and North Dakota who had done just that. What a sorry sight to see your old wheeling buddies having to hoof it around town.

The trail to where the Toyota flipped was pretty sloped. Cameron speculated that Zach had been driving along the ridge and had hit a boulder or bump, and over he went. The closer they got, the less serious the accident looked to him.

There were a couple of boys milling around the truck, scratching their heads, no doubt, about how to right the truck. Two girls in bikinis were walking up from the other side of the trail, local looky-loos. A girl, Brianna, no doubt, was talking on a cell phone, waving her hands in the air for emphasis.

The boys saw Cameron first, and one started to run toward his Jeep. The cavalry had arrived. He paused for only a moment when he saw Mike in the passenger seat, but then ran even faster.

The tall, lanky kid with golden hair was breathless from running and nervousness, no doubt. "Bishop! Man, am I glad to see you, and in a Jeep with a winch no less."

"Zach." Mike spoke soberly. "So what happened, who's hurt?"

"Hurt?" Zachary looked surprised. "No one's hurt. We just tipped the Toyota."

"Brianna said there were kids hurt."

Zachary shook his head violently. "No. No one's hurt. I was the one driving, and I'm fine, a little mad at myself but not hurt. Brianna overreacts."

"Brianna seems to think there were more of you in the Toyota when it rolled over." Mike was both relieved and angry. It was great that they were all okay, but it was going to take a while for him to release all the adrenaline pumping in his system, thanks to these numbskull kids.

"She's a little confused." Zachary shook his head while rolling his eyes. "Just before I rolled over, we had a couple of kids in the truck, but they got out. I decided to take one last ride, and I took a boulder too fast and tipped it over. All things considered, it was actually pretty cool." He nodded his head and grinned.

Cameron liked this guy already.

"Zach, this is Cameron, my nephew from Kentucky. This is his Jeep."

Zachary reached a hand up toward Cameron. "Nice rig."

"Thanks. I'm pretty sure we can get you righted in a bit. I was looking at the space between those trees and if I get her . . ." he said, referring to his Jeep, "back between that rock and your 'Yoda', I should be able to pull her up."

"Oh, right. I can see what you mean. Are you going to want us on the other side?"

"I don't think so, but why don't you hop in, and we'll check it out."

Zachary threw his legs over the back of the Jeep and belted himself in. Cameron drove his Jeep closer to the Toyota. Easy stuff, he thought.

The bikini-clad girls were talking to the other boys. Brianna recognized Mike in the Jeep and ran toward him.

"Bishop!" Brianna exclaimed.

Cameron suddenly realized that they were referring to his Uncle Mike. He wasn't sure why they were calling him that. He thought of bishops being Catholic, and he knew darn well his uncle was Mormon.

"Brianna, I thought you said kids were hurt."

"I did. I mean I thought they were hurt. When I left to go make a phone call, there were a bunch of kids in the truck. When I was coming back down the hill, I saw the truck on its side. I saw Zach and a couple of the other boys lying on the ground looking at something. I couldn't see anyone else, so I thought that was what they were looking at. I ran back up the hill because I figured I could get better reception up there. I called you first. By the time I found out that only Zach was in the truck, you were on your way. I told Stacy, but she said your cell phone didn't work out here. I'm really sorry to have to take you away from family night. I really did think they were hurt. Oh, Stacy said to tell you that Brother Powers is at the top of the trail. Since no one was hurt, he didn't really want to bring his new truck down here.

You're supposed to call his cell phone. He's going to wait there until you call."

"It's okay, Brianna. You just gave me quite a scare." Mike looked down at his cell phone—there was only half a bar of reception showing. "You say I can get reception if I go up the hill a bit?"

"Yeah, you don't have to go very far. I was getting almost three bars up there by that tree," and she pointed to a gnarled oak on the side of the hill.

"Cameron, do you need me?"

"No. I'm good. You go make phone calls."

Mike hopped down from the Jeep and started up the hill.

Out of the corner of his eye, Cameron could see another girl coming down the hill. He didn't have to fully see her to know who it was. He felt her before he saw her face—Lauren.

He didn't know why he was so surprised. If he had thought about it, he might have even anticipated her being here since Brianna was the one who called. Maybe because of the urgency of his coming, he had mentally blocked thinking about her for the time being.

He watched her now as she crawled over a large bolder. She was grace in action, her long, slender legs finding toe holds so she could climb down. She hit the soft dirt with both feet and a puff of dust filled the air around her ankles. She walked toward his Jeep, and he could feel a lump beginning to form in the pit of his stomach.

"Cameron? What a surprise."

"Yeah," was all he said. He thought it was a lame response.

"Hey, Lauren," Zachary said.

Lauren nodded in return, but her focus was on Cameron. "Did Bishop ask you to come help?"

"No, I actually volunteered. I was over there for dinner and family time."

Lauren crinkled her nose for a second. "Oh, family home evening."

"Yeah, something like that."

Zachary jumped out of the Jeep. "Hey, I'm going to go get my towrope."

Cameron gave a nod of agreement, but he wasn't really paying attention to Zach. The truth was, all he needed to right the truck was his winch, but he let Zach go anyway. All of his attention was focused on the girl who was starting to drive him crazy. He turned back to Lauren.

"So what did you think?" Lauren asked.

Cameron's eyebrows furrowed. "About what?" he asked tentatively.

"About family home evening. It would be your first, right?"

"Oh, right. Well, actually it hadn't started quite yet, if you were referring to the lesson. We were just getting ready to eat when Brianna called."

"So you haven't even eaten yet?"

As if on cue, his stomach rumbled. He smiled sheepishly.

"Well, that I can do something about. We were out here for a picnic. Some of us singles get together on Monday nights and have our own family night. We usually go out after each of our own families have theirs. Family home evenings at my house are usually pretty short and sweet because we have a two-year-old." She smiled broadly and continued. "Stacy almost never comes to these, though, because her dad is the bishop, and they do something for the whole night."

"Why is Mike called a bishop?"

"Oh, that's his calling. He's the bishop of the Second Ward. It's sort of like a minister but without the pay."

"Oh."

At that moment Mike came down the hill. "Cameron, I'm going to go meet Brother Powers at the top of the hill." Mike shook his head and rolled his eyes before he spoke again. "He thought he could make it down here but got stuck up near the top of the trail. I am going to walk up and see if I can help him out."

"Do you want me to come too?" Cameron asked.

"No, you stay here and help Zachary. I think that Terry just needs to be guided out of a tight spot." Mike turned and started walking back up the hill, under an umbrella of oaks.

"So," Lauren began again, "do you do this often?"

"What? Pull trucks up? Well, sort of. I don't mind helping, and my Jeep is pretty strong. It actually has more torque than most four-wheel drives."

"What's torque?"

Cameron gritted his teeth. "Well, it's sort of . . ." Cameron twisted his hands in the air, " . . . how much power you have to pull based on horsepower."

Lauren looked puzzled.

"Ah, that's really not a very good description. It just has to do with how much pulling power I have, and my Jeep has a lot."

Lauren nodded. "Okay. Would you like something to eat before you get started?"

"You don't have to do that."

"I know I don't, but I want to. Is that okay?"

"Well, sure. I'll take most anything you have to offer."

"I have half of a Surfin'bird left."

"You have what?" Cameron raised one eyebrow.

"Surfin'bird. It's a sandwich from Beachhut Deli. It's really good, but their sandwiches are big, and I can never finish them. The only problem is you'll have to deal with my cooties." Lauren's eyes sparkled when she said this.

"Your cooties don't bother me, Lauren." He meant to say it as a joke, but it came out way too serious, and he actually blushed.

Lauren looked at him for a long moment and then smiled in return. "All right then, I'll go get it." She turned and walked back toward the big rock she had been sitting on.

Cameron sighed and leaned his head back against the seat. What a dope he was. "Your cooties don't bother me . . ." He shuddered at the remembrance. He watched her climb back up the rock and get her backpack. A second later he realized the girls in the bikinis were gone. That was weird. He loved girls in bikinis, and this time he hadn't even noticed when they left. His guy antenna must be faulty.

Lauren was back as quickly as she had gone.

"So how are you going to get the truck up?"

"Well, I'll probably back into that space between those trees and attach a cable from my winch to the frame on the passenger side of the truck. They usually pop right out. Zach was really lucky. He just flipped on his side. I've seen some really weird rollovers where you know the truck was totaled. This one time, a kid I knew rolled his truck over and crushed the whole cab in. It was totally odd. We used my winch to pull the top of the cab away from the body, but it was still all scrunched up. His windshield opening ended up being only about twelve inches wide. He didn't care. He squeezed in the cab and drove her home." Cameron laughed at the memory.

"Wouldn't that be illegal?" Lauren asked practically.

"Well, sure, but he was only going a few miles. Most guys beat the heck out of their trucks when they four-wheel, but then most guys have a truck for wheeling and one for transportation. I don't have that luxury, so I have to keep my nose pretty clean when I go."

Lauren had unwrapped the remaining part of the sandwich and offered it to him. It had sweet little bite marks on the end. It also had green slices of avocado—yuck.

"You won't mind if I don't eat the avocados, will you?"

"Gosh no. Hand them to me. I'll eat them." She reached out her hand, the band of her CTR ring visible on the inside of her slender finger.

Cameron plucked off the offending green vegetables and placed them one by one in Lauren's outstretched hand.

Even with the avocado gone, it didn't diminish the size of the sandwich. He didn't know quite where to start.

"You won't be able to get your mouth around it, so just start anywhere. It's good no matter what part of the sandwich you bite into."

Just as he got the first big bite into his mouth, Zachary came back. "I think we're ready now. I secured all the stuff and got two towropes. I figure if we winch it up, we can pull her out with one tug."

Cameron smiled, his cheeks bulging with soft French bread, turkey, cream cheese, bacon, lettuce, pickle, and tomato. "Mmmmm" was all he could manage.

Zachary looked at the sandwich and smiled. "Surfin'bird. Good choice. You don't have to talk, man. We've all been there. When you're done with your 'bird' just pull your Jeep around."

Lauren handed Cameron a bottle of water she had just opened. It was not icy cold, which made it easier to drink fast. He gulped down a few swigs and wiped his mouth with the back of his hand.

Lauren reached up and dabbed at his chin with her finger. "Mustard," was all she said.

"Thanks." He wiped around his mouth again in case he had left any other condiments on it. He ran his tongue around his teeth for good measure. Then he took another bite and started the messy process all over again.

"So, you don't wear your CTR ring anymore?"

Why do girls do that? he thought. *Just when you put something in your mouth, they ask a question.* He shook his head and pointed to his mouth in order to mime his inability to speak.

Lauren just smiled.

What the heck? Did she do that on purpose?

She continued to look at him sweetly as he sped up his chewing. He swallowed hard and took another drink from the bottle.

"It's in the glove box, actually."

Cameron had taken the ring shopping with him earlier in the day. He thought the jeweler might take it as a trade-in since they seemed to be so popular around here.

"Oh, then you do still wear it. That really makes me feel better. I felt really, really bad after we talked at the restaurant. I didn't mean to get you so upset about a ring that was obviously special to you."

Cameron wiped his face again. For some reason he didn't correct her. He just took another bite, at which time Lauren spoke again—naturally. "So, how's California treating you so far? Any luck with a job? How are you getting on with your grandmother? I really like her. I've known her as long as I've known Stacy. She's over there a lot."

Cameron rolled his eyes this time.

Lauren laughed. "Oh, sorry. I'll bet you think I do that on purpose."

Cameron nodded rapidly in reply, smiling as he did so.

Lauren looked at him, turned slightly away, and started to giggle.

Cameron's eyebrows met in the center with a questioning grimace.

Lauren then reached down into her backpack and pulled out some crumpled napkins. "More mustard," she said as she handed him the wad.

He wiped his chin again.

"Actually, it's on your nose." She turned away from him to contain her laughter.

He quickly wiped at his nose. Then he folded the napkin to what he thought was a clean side and wiped from his forehead to his neck.

This made Lauren laugh even harder. "Stop. You're killing me."

She grabbed the napkins back from him and refolded them. "Let me do it. You're getting it all over your face now." She stepped a little closer to him and gently wiped his forehead, cheek, and the side of his nose. He involuntarily took in a sharp, deep breath when she touched him. To make matters worse, she smelled really nice. A faint hint of perfume lingered in the air as she stepped back.

"Okay, all done. You can keep eating and I'll be on napkin patrol."

"I'm not sure I want to keep eating. I'm obviously not doing such a good job."

"Oh, it's not you. Really. These sandwiches are really messy."

"That would explain the mustard in your hair."

"What?" Lauren reached for her hair with both hands. "Where?" she said as she rapidly patted her head and pulled at her hair.

Cameron started to laugh out loud. "Gotcha."

Lauren stopped patting and narrowed her eyes at him. "Oh, you are so dead."

Cameron shrugged his shoulders. "Sorry," he said unrepentantly.

"Mister, if I . . . " She was interrupted by a shout from Zach.

They both looked toward the overturned truck. Zach was waving his hands for them to hurry up.

Cameron handed the sandwich back to Lauren. "I've got to go to work, but I'll . . . be . . . back," he said in his best Terminator imitation.

Lauren laughed and shook her head. "I'd keep the day job if I were you."

"Oh yeah? Well, well . . . " Cameron couldn't come up with a snappy retort and just let the words fall away.

Lauren's eyebrows raised. "Well, you'll what, mustard boy?"

Cameron opened and closed his mouth in mock indignation. He was still tongue-tied, so he just shook his head and walked toward the truck.

Getting the Toyota upright was the easy part. Getting it running was a bit harder. It coughed and whined when they first started it up. Blue smoke came billowing out of the muffler. Engine oil had gotten into the spark plugs, and the truck was not running on all six cylinders. It had a bad knock.

"What do you think?" Zach asked Cameron.

"Well, at least the engine didn't seize. I think it's going to be okay, but at the very least you're going to have to change the oil and plugs."

"Should I try and drive it out of here?"

Cameron sighed in deep thought. "I don't know. I think so. Well," Cameron looked toward the sky, trying to pull the right answer from the clouds. "I think the best thing to do is to try and get her back up the hill and reassess the situation, if we can keep her running fine. If not, we can hook her to my rig and pull her up. If we hook up now and I go first, I can keep her from straining too much." Cameron slapped at his neck—a mosquito. The sun was rapidly setting. "We better do it fast, though, before we lose any more light."

"Okay." Zach turned to Lauren. "I'd feel better if you rode with Cameron."

"Sure," was Lauren's quick reply, and she hopped in the front seat of his Jeep like she belonged there.

Brother Powers had finally gotten his truck unstuck and offered to drive the other singles back to their cars. Mike offered to stay, but Cameron told him to go home and finish the steaks. He'd be along in while. Now it was just Zach, Cameron, and Lauren. And why Lauren had stayed, Cameron wasn't sure. She told Mike she needed to stay to show Cameron the way back to the Richards home, but Zach could have done that.

Cameron tugged at the towrope that he had hooked from his Jeep to the Toyota. It seemed secure enough. Zach had gotten into his noisy, rocking truck. They were ready to go.

Lauren had stayed pretty quiet while Cameron worked on Zach's truck. She just watched from a nearby rock. Occasionally, she had come over to where they were working and offered them water, but once they had taken it, she had slipped back to her pedestal to observe.

Cameron climbed into his Jeep and smiled at Lauren. She smiled back. Once she was belted in, he wrapped his right arm around the back of her seat and watched the Toyota for a signal to go.

Zach put his truck in gear and slowly started to move. Zach gave a thumbs up. Cameron slid his body around rapidly, shifted gears, and took his foot off the clutch. He wanted to stay a bit ahead of Zach. He didn't want to pull him, but he had to make sure that Zach didn't run over the towrope, either. It was a delicate operation, and he was glad that Lauren continued to be quiet. He needed to concentrate.

Slowly they edged up the hill. Zach's Toyota was holding its own. Cameron was just there for backup. At the top of the hill, Cameron motioned for Zach to stop. He didn't need to pull him down the grade.

Cameron got out and unhooked the towrope from the front end of Zach's truck. He left it attached to his Jeep but just threw the excess onto his back seat and climbed back in. He started to descend the hill toward the equestrian staging grounds. Zach was right behind him. It wasn't quite dark yet, but under the cover of the oaks and with night falling over the foothills, they had both turned on their headlights.

Cameron had been there almost two hours. It was past nine.

He stopped in the parking lot and waited for Zach to pull up beside him.

"Why don't I follow you now?" Cameron offered.

"Good idea. Would you mind following me home?"

"Not at all. How far are you?"

"Not far at all, less than a mile."

"Okay. You lead, but if you get in any trouble just flash your emergency lights and I'll stop."

Zach pulled in front of Cameron's Jeep and headed down the hill. Zach turned to the right, up a dirt road before they even got to Auburn-Folsom road. Zach's Toyota was coughing and shaking like an old lady with pneumonia. A quarter mile up the road, he pulled into a circular gravel driveway. Home.

Zach got out of his Toyota and came around to Cameron's Jeep. He held out his hand. "Thanks, man. I couldn't have done it without you."

Cameron shook his outstretched hand. "No problem. Listen, you're going to need some help with that engine, so why don't I stop by tomorrow after work? I could be here by about six."

"Seriously?"

"Sure. I'd be glad to help. Can you get some new plugs and oil?"

"Are you kidding? Of course I can. Do I need anything else?"

"Probably oil and air filters. Whatever you normally use. I suspect we are going to find a lot of oil where it doesn't belong."

"Okay. Oil, spark plugs, and filters."

"Yeah. Well I've got to go. Oh," Cameron looked at Lauren, "I'm taking you home then, right?"

"Well, I was kind of hoping so. I mean, I thought we'd go to Stacy's first. She can take me home if you can't."

"No, I just didn't know."

"Look, if you have to get home or anything, Stacy can take me home."

Cameron took a deep breath. "No," he said with a bit more finality than he meant.

Both Lauren and Zach looked at him. Lauren had jumped a little, but Zach just smiled and said, "Okay then. See you tomorrow at six."

Cameron gave an acknowledging nod and started his Jeep.

"Do you know how to get back to Mike's?"

"Yes, surprisingly I do. I'm pretty good with directions. Once I've been somewhere I usually can get there again. I don't normally get lost." He backed out of the driveway and headed toward Mike's.

Lauren didn't say much on the trip back until they turned down Mike's street. "I saw you at the mall this afternoon."

"What?" Cameron said with genuine surprise.

"You were at Sears, looking at tools."

Cameron nodded. "You're right, I was. And you were walking by with your boyfriend."

"My boyfriend? Oh no." She smiled at Cameron. "That wasn't my boyfriend."

"The guy you were hanging all over wasn't your boyfriend?" Cameron said teasingly.

"No, the 'guy' I was hanging 'all over' was my brother—my twin brother to be exact. I was helping him pick out a suit. He's leaving on his mission in a month."

Cameron opened his mouth, shut it, opened it again, and then shut it and didn't say a word. He concentrated on pulling into his uncle's driveway instead.

Cameron knocked on the door of his uncle's home. After a moment, Mike answered the door.

"Hey, how'd it go?" Mike said to Cameron, and to Lauren he added, "Thanks for making sure Cameron found his way home."

Lauren nodded, and Cameron spoke. "Zach's truck is going to be fine, I think. I am going to come back up here tomorrow after work to help him get it running. When you roll a truck on its side like that, you usually ruin at least half your spark plugs."

Mike rolled his eyes and smiled. "Yeah, I guess you would. Are you guys hungry? There are some steaks left. They're a little crispy, though."

"No, thanks. Lauren shared her sandwich with me. Where is everyone?"

"Karen took your grandmother home, and the kids went with her. I suspect they're all going out for ice cream too."

"Now ice cream sounds good," said Cameron.

Lauren spoke for the first time. "Well, why don't I take you to Mel's then? I get a discount, and they have the best ice cream in town."

"Uh, okay, sure. I'd love to get some," Cameron stuttered a bit.

"Well, you kids go along then. I have tons of paperwork I'm sorting through, so I am sure that Lauren is going to be much better company."

"Hey, thanks for the offer of steaks, though. Can I take a rain check?"

"Cameron, soon enough I hope you will learn that eating here is a standing offer. You will never need an invitation. We're family and you're a part of that now."

Cameron felt a little catch in his throat and didn't reply at first, but nodded in return. He was just not used to the generosity of his uncle. Actually, he was not used to the generosity of all the people he had encountered in California. So far, he could honestly say, this was the friendliest state he had ever been to.

"Uncle Mike," he started, "well, thanks. I really appreciate all you've done for me so far."

"No problem at all Cameron. Like I said, we're family now. Now go get some ice cream."

Cameron and Lauren smiled, turned, and headed back toward the Jeep.

They were heading down Douglas Boulevard before either of them spoke again. Tonight Lauren had been unusually quiet.

"So tell me about yourself. I mean, all I really know is that you're a Mormon and you work at Mel's."

"What do you want to know?"

"Oh, I don't know. I'm fishing here, trying to make polite conversation." He turned his head briefly from watching the road to smile at her.

"Well, I'm nineteen. I have a twin brother, which I already told you. I also have four younger brothers. I also have a two-year-old nephew that lives with us."

"A two-year-old nephew? One of your younger brothers is married?" Cameron was trying to do the math, and it wasn't adding up.

Lauren blushed in embarrassment. "No, he's not married. It's sort of awkward. My younger brother got his girlfriend pregnant. She was going to have an abortion, and my brother and parents tried to talk her into giving the baby up for adoption. She said no, the only way she would have the baby was if my brother kept him. So my eighteen-year-old brother has a two-year-old son."

"Oh." Cameron didn't know what to say. They were silent for another minute or two. Then Cameron said, "Okay. So how about school?"

Lauren breathed a sigh of relief. This was a subject she could discuss. "I'm at Sierra College right now. I could have gone to BYU, but I wanted to spend this last year with Cale, before he left on his mission."

"Isn't BYU a Mormon college in Utah?"

"Yeah."

"So why didn't you and your brother, what was his name?"

"Cale."

"Okay, why didn't you and Cale both go?"

"He decided to work to save money for his mission."

"Oh, yeah. Souvenirs and side trips."

"Souvenirs and side trips?" Lauren stopped to process what Cameron had said. "Oh, no. He has to pay for his mission. He doesn't need *extra* money. He needs money *for* his mission. They're a bit expensive."

"Wait, doesn't your church pay for your brother's mission?"

"No. He does, or his family, or both."

"You're kidding. So how much is that?"

"I think it's around $10,000 for two years."

"*What*? Ten thousand dollars!"

Lauren smiled and nodded. "It's a big deal for us, Cameron, and most guys and their families fund missions willingly."

"That's the price of a car, or a down payment on a house—well, in Kentucky at least."

"Like I said, it's a big deal to us. Anyway, that's why I'm still at home this year. I am going to BYU in the fall, though. I leave in about four weeks."

"Oh?" Cameron felt an involuntary lump in his chest. Lauren was leaving. *I don't even like her that much*, he thought, but then again the reality of her leaving really bugged him.

"You sound surprised. Didn't think I was the scholarly type, did you?" she teased.

"No, not at all," he said.

"No, as in 'I don't think you're smart'?" Lauren rephrased his response back to him.

"No," Cameron shook his head, "that's not what I meant. I meant, I wasn't surprised that you were smart."

"'*Were* smart?'" Lauren raised her eyebrows in mock indignation.

"*Are* smart? Wait a second, you're driving me crazy on purpose aren't you?"

"Uh-huh. It's my job."

"Well, you deserve a raise, 'cause you're dang good at it."

"You need to turn left here," Lauren said.

Cameron made a quick lane change and cut off a Taurus, which honked at him.

"Hey, speed racer, calm down," Lauren chided Cameron.

"Sorry. I'm still getting used to all the traffic around here," Cameron said sheepishly as he made the left into the parking lot. The place was packed, and they had to park in the back by a bank.

Matthew was the host. Cameron remembered him from the day before.

"Hey, Lauren."

"Hey, Matt. This is my friend, Cameron, from Kentucky."

Matthew reached out his hand to shake Cameron's. His CTR ring was a wide band of silver with black lettering. Cameron couldn't miss it.

"Mormon?" Cameron asked.

"Yeah. You?"

"Gosh no. My relatives are though."

"He's Stacy's cousin," Lauren added in explanation.

Matthew nodded his head and ran his hand through his closely cut hair. "Table or booth?"

"Booth, please," Lauren and Cameron said in unison—then laughed.

Matthew showed them to the same booth they had sat in when they first met. Spooky, Cameron thought.

"So what's good?" Cameron asked Lauren as he looked over the menu.

"It's all good, but we seem to sell the most of the Chocolate Cow sundaes."

"Then, that's what I'll have."

"Good choice."

"So, I have a question? Why do so many Mormons work here?"

Lauren shrugged her shoulders. "I don't know. It's been like that as long as I can remember. The people who own this aren't Mormons, but a lot of us do work here. I think it's nothing more then friends getting friends jobs. I don't think that it's any Mormon conspiracy."

"So, Matt seems like a likable guy. You ever date him?"

"Date Matt? No, he doesn't date."

"What? Why not? Don't tell me it's some Mormon thing." Cameron paused for a moment. "Hey, you don't have arranged marriages or anything do you? I mean, I heard about the polygamy thing—but I thought you didn't do that anymore."

"No, the 'polygamy thing' is over. Matt doesn't date because he is going on a mission, and he doesn't want to get involved."

"Involved?"

"Yeah. Personally, I think he takes *not* dating to the extreme, but to each his own."

"So you would date him if he asked?"

"I don't know. I suppose, but that's not going to happen. He's leaving before I do. He's going to Boise."

"Where's Boise?"

"It's in Idaho. My brother is going to Brazil."

"Oh, does your brother speak Portuguese?"

"Not yet. They'll teach him at the MTC in Brazil."

"What's an MTC?"

"Mission Training Center. Missionaries go there first to learn the discussions and a language if they are going foreign."

"So is Matt paying for his own mission too?"

"Yes. Matt and his parents."

"Wow. That just boggles the mind. It's such a big commitment."

"Exactly. That's probably what makes missionaries so effective. They're committed. They actually put their money where their mouths are."

"People in our church go on missions too."

"Which church?" Lauren winked at him.

"Oh, don't even start with me Mormon girl!" Cameron laughed.

"Just kidding. I know other churches send out missionaries. It's not a new thing. It's as old as the first apostles."

"I don't think I could go on a mission at this age."

"How old are you?"

"Twenty. I'll be twenty-one on Wednesday, actually."

"This Wednesday, as in the day after tomorrow?"

"Yeah."

"So how are you going to celebrate? Are you going to go out drinking?"

"I doubt it. I've actually never been a drinker. My dad was an alcoholic. It bugged the crap out of me. I don't drink—period. As for my actual birthday, it's not that big of a deal to me." Cameron shrugged his shoulders.

"I find that hard to believe. Every guy I know makes a big deal out of turning twenty-one, drinkers or not."

"Well, I'm not like every guy you know."

"I noticed," Lauren said softly.

Cameron sensed that there seemed to be some undercurrent to this conversation that he didn't understand.

Lauren continued. "So on Wednesday, why don't you meet me here at Mel's about nine, and I'll treat you to a birthday sundae and more stimulating conversation?"

"Are you asking me out?" Cameron challenged her straight up.

"Uh, no. Well, maybe. I guess it looks that way." Lauren's face turned bright pink. "But if it makes you feel any better, I'm not really going to spend much on our 'date.' Everyone gets a free sundae on their birthday. You don't need to eat one with me to get it."

"Oh, I see how it is. So that's all I'm worth to you." He smiled broadly as he spoke.

"Cameron, now you're driving me crazy. Do you want the sundae or not?"

"Of course I do, but only if I have it with you."

"Then fine. Be here at nine. It won't be so crowded."

"Can we go to a movie afterward?" Cameron said naturally, and it surprised him a little how right it felt.

"Uh . . ." Lauren's mouth just hung open, and her eyes popped wide. She sat motionless in this position.

Cameron reached across the table and put one finger on her top lip and his thumb on her bottom lip. He gently closed her mouth. "What? It's okay for you to ask me out, but I can't return the favor?"

"No." Lauren paused. "It's just. . . well . . . this is going to sound kind of stupid seeing as I just asked you out and all . . . but . . . well . . ."

"For Pete's sake, Lauren, spit it out."

"It's just that I've never actually dated someone who isn't Mormon."

Cameron didn't skip a beat. "And I've never actually dated someone who is. So does that make it complicated for you? The fact that I'm not a Mormon?"

"Maybe," Lauren replied slowly.

"You've never been asked out by guys who weren't Mormon? I find that hard to believe."

"No, I've been asked out," Lauren said.

"Plenty of times, I'll bet," Cameron said.

Lauren shrugged her shoulders and avoided Cameron's eyes in distinct embarrassment. "Not as much as you seem to think, I'm sure."

"So what do you say to them? I mean, how do you turn them down?" Cameron felt himself getting a little agitated.

"I'm not rude, if that's what you mean." Lauren insisted.

"No," Cameron sighed. "I doubt if you are ever rude to anyone on purpose. I just really want to know how you break it to them. Do you actually say 'I can't go out with you because you're not Mormon'?" Cameron knew he was pushing her, but for some reason this was a really important question for him.

"Not in so many words," Lauren said, starting to get confused.

"So what words do you use?" Cameron locked eyes with Lauren.

Lauren blinked and turned her head slightly to avoid his gaze. "I'm not sure why you are so interested in this."

"I just find it weird that for a sweet Mormon girl you can be so judgmental at times."

Lauren huffed in response. "I am not judgmental."

"Well, what do you call it? When we first met, what did you think about me? You thought I was a 'fallen' Mormon. You didn't know a thing about me, but you decided it was your Mormon duty to put me in my place."

"Ouch," was all Lauren could say.

"So you don't deny it?"

"Well, not when you put it that way. But I don't think of myself as judgmental. I prefer to think of myself as open."

"Open?" Cameron said with a bit of incredulity in his voice.

"Yes. Open—as in honest."

"Okay then, how do you honestly tell a guy who's interested in you that he's not worthy because he's not Mormon?"

"I think you're twisting what I meant."

"So untwist it. What *do* you say?"

Lauren shifted uneasily on her side of the booth. "Well, before I was sixteen it was easy. My parents didn't let me date. After sixteen I had to get a bit more creative."

"And?"

"And it depended on who asked. I mean there were different answers for different situations," Lauren said.

"Wait a sec. Isn't there just one answer? 'I don't date non-Mormons.'"

"I suppose that is the underlying reason, but I don't want to hurt anyone's feelings, so I'm a bit more gentle than that."

"Okay, so now we're back to my original question. How do you tell someone you're not willing to date him? Does the subject of your religion even come up?"

"Not usually," Lauren said.

"Aha!" Cameron said in a short, loud burst of emotion. The people at the table across from theirs looked at them both.

"Aha what?" Lauren almost whispered in return.

"Aha, you are not being honest then."

"Look, you can be honest without being brutal or rude."

"Okay, so tell me what words do you use?"

"Well, maybe I just say I'm not available that night and then I make sure I'm not."

"What? That seems pretty deceptive to me."

"Why? If I say I can't go out on Friday because I am doing something with my family and then I do something with my family, I was honest and I didn't hurt anyone's feelings."

"So what about when he asks you out a second or third time?" Cameron asked.

"If I am always busy, he usually gets the idea I'm not available."

"Especially if he sees you out with some Mormon dude the next Friday night."

"So? What would you rather me do? Say 'I can't go out with you because you're not Mormon, and I only want to date guys I could potentially marry?'"

"Sure. Why not? At least that would be the truth."

"In this case the truth may be overrated," Lauren said.

"When is the truth ever wrong?" Cameron asked angrily. He was thinking about his mother's recent revelations about his father being a Mormon.

"When it hurts someone's feelings."

"But your lack of truth is just as potentially painful."

"I don't lie, Cameron. I do what I do to spare feelings."

Cameron didn't respond. He took a long drink of water and stared out the window at the cars passing by.

The silence was awkward. Lauren took a sip of her water and

twiddled with the hair on the nape of her neck.

Matthew walked up to the table. He was in the process of seating another couple in the booth next to theirs. He looked at Lauren, then at Cameron, then back to Lauren. He raised his eyebrows and shoulders questioningly. Lauren closed her eyes and shook her head in response.

Cameron finally broke the silence. "So asking me out was a freak accident." It was more of a statement than a question.

"Well, I wouldn't use the term 'freak,' but yes, I guess so. Actually, I wasn't thinking of it as 'asking you out' until you brought it up. I was just trying to be friendly to the new guy in town."

"I don't need your sympathy," Cameron spit out bitterly. "I get enough of that from my mother."

"Hey, I don't feel sorry for you. And besides you turned around and asked me out. Why'd you do that if you hate Mormons so much?"

"That was before I knew your rules," Cameron said.

"That's not fair. You would never have been aware of my rules if you weren't so, so pushy."

"Pushy? Me? I don't think so. You're the one with the defective open-policy problem," Cameron said.

Lauren winced in pain.

"The truth hurts doesn't it?" Cameron said.

Cameron was getting frustrated at how Lauren was now trying to make him out to be the bad guy.

"Exactly, Cameron. Sometimes brutal honesty can be very painful. I think I mentioned that before." Lauren felt hot tears welling up in her eyes. She tried blinking rapidly to stop them from running down her cheeks. "Maybe that's why I am careful *not* to be so brutally honest with nonmembers who ask me out."

Cameron turned and looked out the window again.

Lauren spoke. "I'm not hungry anymore. Can you just take me home?"

"Fine." Cameron slid out from his side of the booth and pulled the keys out of his pocket. He took a deep breath. He hadn't realized how tired he was—exhausted actually—and he needed to start his new job in the morning.

Luckily, Lauren didn't live far away. She lived in a nondescript suburban neighborhood. The houses were newer and had that cookie-cutter feel. It was dark enough that he probably wouldn't be able to find her house again, which was fine by him.

TUESDAY

The initial awkwardness of work didn't last long. By noon Cameron was welding parts on a red Chevy Blazer without direct supervision. Roland, his new boss, was generous but demanding. He expected new employees to hit the pavement running.

Fortunately, Cameron was not afraid of physical work, and by lunchtime he had found a comfortable pace that worked for both him and Roland. He had to admit, though, that he was staying hyper-focused on work in order to block out last night.

Not only did the whole Mel's thing with Lauren leave a bad taste in his mouth, he had also been stopped by a Roseville police officer for speeding.

Evidently, in his growing anger toward Lauren not wanting to date him because he wasn't Mormon, he had tensed up and pushed a bit too hard on the accelerator.

The officer had taken his North Dakota license and discussed with him the finer points of being in California now. He also told Cameron to get a California driver's license if he planned on staying.

Cameron was more than polite and "yes, sir'd" and "no, sir'd" the officer to death.

It was nothing short of divine intervention that he had not gotten a ticket. He was doing almost seventy in a fifty mile per hour zone. He drove five miles under the posted speed limit the rest of the way home. His grandmother was, of course, sound asleep when he arrived. He fell into bed exhausted and slept fitfully. He was up and on his way to work by seven the next morning.

He hadn't had much time to talk to Rock, which worked for him anyway. He didn't want to go back to The Arm of Christ church anytime soon.

At 12:30 Roland told him to break for lunch. It was weird walking into work this morning with a little brown lunch sack full of homemade goodness, but he got over his embarrassment when he bit into the sweet, freshly baked whole wheat bread and turkey sandwich. His grandmother had also included a bunch of grapes, a can of root beer, and a tiny bag of potato chips. Cute.

He smiled at the sweetness of the gesture, but it was also confusing to him. The woman he knew as his grandmother was the same person his father called Mom. She was the same mother his father had left to pursue a life far from her and her religion. He kneaded his thumb and forefinger on his temple. He didn't understand so many things.

As he sat in his Jeep, which he preferred over the break room, his thoughts wandered back to last night. Once his anger had dissipated, he had a sick feeling in the pit of his stomach. He had really hurt Lauren.

Why had he been so cruel?

He thought back to relationships he had had with other girls over the years, and he could honestly say that he had never made a girl cry—unless he counted his mother.

Lauren got under his skin. Every time he was near her he felt . . . what? What did he feel? That was what bothered Cameron the most. It was as if her soul or spirit or whatever you wanted to call it was bigger than her physical body. A soft, golden light spilled out of her, and he was being drawn toward it like a moth to a porch light on a Kentucky summer night.

But he couldn't actually get to the light, so he just kept bumping up against it. He got more frustrated with each attempt.

It occurred to him that in the three days he had been in California, he had seen Lauren each day—more by happenstance than by design.

He crumpled his chip bag into a tight, noisy wad and tossed it into his empty lunch sack. The drained soda can went in next. He still had forty-five minutes left of his lunch hour.

He started his Jeep. As he passed by an open auto bay, Rock nodded at him. Cameron nodded back.

In less than ten minutes, he was on Douglas Boulevard passing Mel's. Fifteen minutes into his drive, he found himself turning down a street less than fourteen hours earlier he had sworn he would forget.

He drove by her house.

He didn't stop, at least not right in front of it. He went to the next intersection and doubled back.

He parked, with his motor running, three houses and seven trees away. He was pretty sure that anyone in the house would not be able to see him.

He sat staring at her home for exactly five minutes. He knew this because he kept looking at his watch. He knew he couldn't get out and talk to her because he had to get back to work. He also knew he had to see her again and apologize.

In a quick burst of impulsiveness, he pulled directly in front of the sleepy house. He reached over and popped open his glove box.

Inside were his CTR ring and his pack of cigarettes. When he reached for the CTR ring, his cigarettes fell under the seat. He made a mental note to put them back when he got to work.

With the engine still humming, he hopped down from his Jeep. In three quick, long strides, he was at her front porch.

He only hesitated a moment before laying the size twelve ring on the front mat.

Less than thirty seconds later, a neighbor of Lauren's peered from her window to see what adolescent idiot was peeling out down the street. She didn't recognize the Jeep.

"Gramma Clara?" Cameron hesitated a moment on the phone before he continued talking to his grandmother. "This is Cameron, your grandson."

"Cameron, I actually know who you are. I may seem old, but I'm not senile yet."

"No, I didn't mean to imply . . ."

Clara laughed. "Cameron, I'm just kidding with you. How was your first day at work?"

"Good," Cameron said. "I was put straight to work, so it went by fast. Oh, and by the way, the lunch was great. Thanks so much."

"Was it enough?"

"It was great, really," Cameron repeated.

"Would you like me to make lunches for you everyday?"

"Oh, you don't have to do that."

"I know I don't, but I want to."

"Well then, sure."

"So are you on your way home? We are having leftovers that Karen sent home with me from the barbecue last night."

"No, actually, that's what I was calling about. I'm still at work, but I am going over to help that kid who rolled his truck last night."

"That's awfully nice of you to help Zach," Clara said.

Cameron was surprised his grandmother knew Zach's name. "It's no big deal, really. I don't know when I'll be home, though."

"I'll leave the light on for you. Now you go have fun."

"Thanks, although I don't know how much fun it's going to be."

"Well, I expect it will be more fun than sitting home and watching the weather channel with a seventy-four-year-old lady."

"You may have me there. My mom always watches the weather channel. I haven't got a clue what the fascination is with that particular form of television programming."

"Me? I've been hooked on it ever since Mike and Karen talked me into getting cable," Clara said.

"All right then, Gramma, have fun." Cameron hung the beige, no-nonsense work phone on its hook.

By six o'clock he was literally up to his elbows in oil and dirt.

Zach's house was a modest yellow clapboard affair on a beautiful piece of land.

Zach had dutifully gotten six Autolite spark plugs, five quarts of 10W-30 oil, and two filters. Working together, they got all the plugs out and cleaned up the spilled engine oil in less than forty minutes.

The rest of the process went pretty quickly. By seven-thirty Cameron was on his back under the Toyota, tightening the oil filter down. He stopped for a moment when he heard the distinct sound of a motorcycle pull up the gravel driveway, but he didn't stop what he was doing. This wasn't his house.

He heard people walking by the Toyota toward the house. A moment later he heard his name.

"Cameron?"

His heart froze. He momentarily forgot he was under the truck and lifted his head right into the driveline. It hit with an audible thud.

"Cameron? Are you okay?" Lauren's voice went up an octave.

He turned his head to see a sandaled pair of feet, with cherry red toenail polish, at the front of the truck. She was so close he could reach one hand out and grab a small, tanned ankle.

"Yeah, I'm okay." He rubbed his forehead with a greasy palm. "Please don't tell me you drove a motorcycle over here."

"Why? You don't think I can drive a motorcycle?" Lauren responded.

"I don't know. I just don't think of you as a biker chick."

"No, I didn't drive. My brother did. I don't have my driver's license yet."

Cameron continued to lie under the truck. He preferred to stay holed up as long as he could. He didn't want to face Lauren after what he had said last night. "Oh."

"So how close are you guys to being done? Or I guess I should say you, since Zach just went in the house with my brother."

"I don't know. A little while yet."

"How much time is a little while?"

"Never can tell," Cameron said evasively.

Lauren didn't say anything for almost a minute. When she did, there were tears in her voice. "Cameron, I know you're mad at me for what I said last night, and I feel so awful. I knew you were going to be over here, so I begged Cale to bring me over so I could apologize in person. I can totally understand if you don't want to see me."

Her voice was so plaintive and broken that Cameron almost cried. He couldn't respond because his throat was getting tighter by the moment.

"Okay then," Lauren finally said, "I completely understand. This was probably a bad idea." She started to move away from the truck.

Cameron still didn't say anything, but he reached out his hand and wrapped his fingers gently around her right ankle. He didn't care that he had oil on them. He didn't care that she probably thought he was weird. He only cared that she stay put.

"Don't go," was all he could whisper.

Lauren stood motionless.

Cameron didn't remove his hand from around Lauren's ankle, and Lauren didn't make an attempt to move. Cameron lay on his back and squeezed his eyes shut. Two tears ran down his face toward each ear. He was biting down on his quivering lower lip. He couldn't believe that Lauren was apologizing *to him*. He knew that this was all his fault. He was the one with hang-ups. She was just a nice Mormon girl who was getting caught in the middle of his own personal crisis. All she wanted to do was practice her religion and hurt as few people as possible in the process.

He gently released his grip on her ankle and let his hand fall open, palm up, on the ground. He wasn't sure what to do or say next. Lauren continued to hold her position.

Then Lauren shuffled her feet and repositioned herself. She knelt down and reached for Cameron's outstretched hand. She had to maneuver a little awkwardly to get her fingers intertwined with his, but once she did she held on tightly.

Cameron began to shake all over slightly. This was the last thing he expected. His hand shook within her tiny hand. She used her other hand to stroke the top of the quivering hand she currently held. She lightly touched the pale skin on Cameron's hand where his CTR ring used to be.

"I don't understand," Cameron said at last. "I thought for sure you hated me."

"I don't hate you." She squeezed his hand tighter for emphasis. "The thought that you might be thinking that is what has driven me crazy ever since you dropped me off last night. I have been sick with worry, and I mean literally sick. I haven't eaten a thing since that Surfin'bird last night. Then when Cale came home from work this afternoon, he brought your ring in from the porch. Of course he didn't know it was your ring, he just thought it was weird that someone left a CTR ring on our doorstep. I recognized it right away and took it. My mom keeps asking me why someone would leave a perfectly good CTR ring on a doormat. I just avoided her. Number one, I don't actually know why you did, and number two, she can be a little bit nosy at times. I mean, don't get me wrong, I love my mom, but she wants to know every little thing that goes on in my life. I haven't really told her about you yet. Gosh, I'm talking too much aren't I?"

"No," was all Cameron said. He found her voice very soothing. His heart rate was evening out, and his breathing was more normal.

The shaking was almost gone. He was still afraid to look at Lauren, though.

"Well, anyway, like I said, I begged Cale to bring me over here. He didn't want to at first, so I had to bribe him. I actually had to pay him five dollars—do you believe that?" She laughed a little and continued to hold his hand.

"I could pay you back," Cameron said weakly.

"That's not what I meant. I didn't mind paying the five. I have gotten my money's worth already. But he is such a little money-grubber."

Cameron didn't want to speak. He didn't want to break the spell. He just wanted to lay on the gravel driveway, with Lauren holding his hand and chattering at him. "Mmm," was all he said.

"Are you going to come out from under that truck anytime soon? My knees are starting to hurt a little."

"Oh, sorry. I was actually just finishing up. Hold on." Cameron had to pull his hand away from Lauren's in order to pull himself out. Letting go of her was the single most painful thing he had done since arriving in California. She moved around to the side of the truck where he was exiting.

He smiled an awkward smile at her. She smiled back. He got himself up to a sitting position but didn't stand. She bent down again to his level. She had oil on both hands and one ankle. She reached toward his face and gently wiped where the tears had recently traveled. His hand stopped her small, cool hand on his cheek. He put his fingers around hers and closed his eyes again. "Lauren, you're killing me."

"I know."

"Why?" Cameron asked sincerely.

"I don't know. I don't know what's happening," Lauren replied.

"I've only known you for three days."

"I know," Lauren said.

"I'm not a Mormon."

"I know," Lauren said.

He opened his eyes slowly and looked into hers, more than slightly confused.

A screen door slammed nearby. Lauren pulled her hand away from Cameron's cheek and stood up. Cameron quickly rubbed his face with the back of his hand to erase any signs of emotion and pulled himself upright also.

Zach and Cale were walking toward the truck.

When they reached the Toyota, Lauren and Cameron were standing miles apart from each other compared to where they had just been.

"Done," Cameron said to Zach. "I think we can start her up."

"Cool." Zach looked at Lauren. "Whoa, look at your hands." He turned to Cameron. "What did you have her doing? Changing the oil?"

Cameron looked at Lauren and winked. "Yeah, something like that. What was I supposed to do? You bugged out. I had to have someone to help."

"Lauren," Cale chimed in, "I can see how you might get the oil on your hands, but how in the world did you get it on your ankle? What a dweeb."

"Spoken like a true brother." Lauren smiled at Cale. Then she looked at her ankle and shook her head in mock confusion. "I'm just not cut out for this kind of work, I guess."

"Yeah, stick to the ice cream, Lauren," Zach added.

"Good idea," Lauren agreed.

Thankfully, the truck started the first time. It was smoking a little bit, but that was normal after a rollover. Oil tended to get on the outside of the engine, and as the engine heated up, it would smoke and smell rather bad.

"Cameron, you are a lifesaver," Zach said. "I was so afraid I had really messed up my truck this time."

"I think your truck is going to be fine."

"Lauren, I got to get home," Cale said impatiently.

"Uh, I can take her home, if you're in a hurry," Cameron said.

Cale shrugged his shoulders. "It's up to you," he said to his sister.

"I think I'll ride with Cameron."

"Okay." He headed toward his motorcycle.

Cameron turned to Zach. "Are you going to be okay?"

"Sure. I'm just going to take it easy for a few days to make sure I didn't break anything else. I'm not that concerned about the dents. It's an old truck and as long as the doors open and close, I'm good."

"Okay then, I think we are going to take off. Well, actually, we need a sink to clean up in first."

"We have a utility sink in the garage. I think we even have some of that orange goop mechanics like. My dad bought a tub of it last month."

"Perfect. Lauren, after you." Cameron motioned for her to lead the way.

They got most of the oil off of their hands. Cameron got quite a bit off his face, and Lauren's ankle was almost as good as new.

Lauren was in the Jeep before Cameron.

"Where to?" Cameron asked.

"Do you want to go eat?" Lauren asked.

"I was hoping you would say that. I'm starving."

"Mel's?" Lauren asked.

"Uh, no. I'm a little too dirty to go there. Let's try somewhere else."

"Like where?" Lauren asked.

"I don't know. A drive-through or something."

"We could go the grocery store and share some Chinese food. We could eat it out by the lake."

"Okay, I like Chinese," Cameron said.

They picked up a broccoli-beef combination plate and an egg roll at the Chinese deli. The clerk added to the bag—paper plates, napkins, chopsticks, and one fortune cookie. Cameron got a Kiwi-Strawberry Snapple; Lauren got a Cranberry-Grapefruit Sobe.

The grocery store was close to the lake. It was after 7:30, so there was no one at the tollbooth. They didn't have to pay the entrance fee. They just drove into the state park. The tourist crowds were gone. It was mostly just local people who were pulling boats out of the water.

"Where to?" Cameron asked.

"You kind of like dirt trails, right?"

"Sure."

"Well, if you go down here a while, eventually the asphalt ends and the trails are all dirt. There aren't boulders or anything, but they have ruts and stuff. It may fulfill your need to four-wheel, and we can get right next to the lake."

Cameron followed the paved road until it ended. He got on the dirt road but didn't need to put his Jeep in four-wheel drive. He drove a bit longer and pulled his truck right onto the shoulder of the lake.

They were both quiet as they sat in the truck to eat. Cameron was finished with his half of the meal first.

"You aren't going to get in trouble or anything for being out here with me are you?" Cameron asked as he wadded up his trash to put in the grocery sack.

"No, and I have my cell phone with me. If my mom wants me, you can be sure she'll call."

"Okay." He stared at the lake in awkward silence. *Now what?* he thought.

When Lauren had finished all but the Sobe, she handed the single fortune cookie to Cameron. He refused it.

"I think you should have it. It was your idea to get Chinese," he said.

"But we only have one fortune cookie, and you're new in town."

"Well, we'll share it then, okay?" He took the cookie out of the cellophane wrapper and broke it in half. He pulled the fortune out. "We'll read it together," he said as he leaned over toward Lauren.

"You will go on exciting trip," Lauren read for both of them. She shook her head and laughed. "You would think that they could get English-speaking people to write these things, or at least correct the grammar."

"Who believes these things anyway?" Cameron asked. He turned the fortune over to reveal the lottery numbers on the back. "Do you think anyone has actually won a lottery using these numbers?"

"I doubt it."

"It cracks me up what some people use to guide their lives."

"You mean like astrology?"

"Exactly. Horoscopes, numerology, bumps on their heads, fortune tellers—all a bunch of scam artists."

"I agree. They certainly aren't being lead by the Spirit."

"Right." Cameron's voice trailed off. He wanted to ask Lauren a question about her belief in the Holy Spirit but was afraid of getting into an argument again.

"What?" Lauren looked at him through narrowed eyes.

"What, what?" Cameron widened his eyes in return.

"You were going to say something else. What?"

"No, I wasn't. I was just agreeing with you."

"You liar," Lauren said teasingly. "I can tell you weren't done. Spit it out."

"I don't want to. I don't want us to argue."

"Cameron, I agree that we have gotten into a couple of heated discussions, but if we don't learn to talk back and forth, then what good is there in going out?"

She said "going out" so casually, like it was a real possibility, that Cameron jumped a little in his seat.

"Now what?" Lauren asked.

"Lauren, the truth is, I do have a question and part of me wants to ask you, but another part of me is scared of you."

"Scared of me?" Lauren's voice tightened.

"You sound surprised."

"A little. I don't think anyone has ever told me I was scary."

"You can be. You have such strong convictions, and you're not afraid to share them. You speak with an openness that can be a bit intimidating."

"You make that sound bad," Lauren said softly.

"Not bad, so much as, well, I think maybe people feel like they can't meet your expectations. I know I can't."

"Cameron, I feel so awful about the other night. I already told you that."

"I know you do. And the weird thing is that I am the one who should be apologizing to you. I was the jerk. I pushed you into a corner, like an animal, and then dared you to bite. You did, and I got angry. How fair was that?"

"Maybe we were both to blame. Can't we just start over?"

"I don't think we can start over. Maybe we can go on from here, but we have both said a lot of things that still need to be resolved."

"Okay, I'm willing to work on this if you are. We can start with you telling me what you held back a few minutes ago."

Cameron had to close his eyes to remember what he was going to ask. "Oh, I remember. It was about the Holy Spirit, actually. I wondered what Mormons think about him."

"Well, first, we call him the Holy Ghost, but I am sure we are speaking of the same member of the Godhead. What exactly did you want to know?"

"Just if your church believes in him."

"Of course we believe in him. How could we be a Christian church and not believe in the Holy Ghost?" Lauren asked.

"Oh, different churches put emphasis on different things. Some are really into Mary, for example. Some are focused exclusively on Jesus. Some churches preach the wonders of the Holy Spirit. Where does the Holy, uh, Ghost fit into your religion?" Cameron asked.

"We see him as a member of the Godhead. There is the Father, Son and Holy Ghost. The Holy Ghost to us is the main conduit between Heavenly Father and his children here on earth. He is the one who guides us. He is the one who provides the personal revelation that people here on earth so desperately need to survive."

"Do you pray to him?"

"Gosh no. We pray to our Heavenly Father in the name of Jesus Christ. The Holy Ghost is the one who whispers the answers back."

"Okay, so far I can accept what you're saying, which may just mean it's not too far off from what I believe. This, incidentally, is a bit surprising to me because I thought we would be farther apart on most issues surrounding religion."

"Cameron, no offence to whoever told you about our church, but I really think if you want to know about Mormons, or the Mormon Church in general, you ought to ask a Mormon."

Cameron shrugged his shoulders. "Probably, and while I could ask my grandmother or Mike even, I am not ready to discuss this with them quite yet. Can I just ask you?"

"Of course you can. It's just that I may not be able to answer all your questions. Also, I depend a lot on the Holy Ghost for what guides me. I may not have the exact scripture reference to back up what I believe."

"Fair enough. I try to listen to the Spirit myself. I pray, you know." He said this last sentence almost defensively.

Lauren reached over and put her hand on top of his. She squeezed it gently.

Cameron closed his eyes. Her hand was so light on his.

"Do you remember the first night we met?" Lauren asked, her hand still resting on Cameron's.

"Of course."

"Something happened that night. I wasn't looking for it, and I can tell neither were you, but I don't think we met by accident."

"You mean fate?"

"Not fate, because fate implies you can't change what is happening. I just think that you were meant to come to California."

"Why?"

Lauren looked away.

"Hey, you can't hold back now."

"I am pretty sure it has something to do with finding the gospel." Lauren quickly added, "Now don't get freaked out. I know you think that Mormons are the evil-children-of-the-devil, but I believe that is just the adversary working on you. I don't think it is coincidence that we met, or that you are related to the Richards family."

Cameron felt a strange feeling wash over him. He couldn't tell if it was in response to what Lauren was saying, or if it was the fact that she squeezed his hand as she said it.

"So I have a question," Cameron started. "Is this a date?"

Lauren smiled. "I think so."

"So what happened to your rule?"

"Suspended for the time being."

"Just like that?"

"Just like that," Lauren said.

"Why?" Cameron asked.

"Because I prayed about it."

"You prayed about . . . about us?" Cameron was shaken by this revelation.

"Not so much 'us' in the beginning. I didn't think I would ever see you again, but to tell the truth, you entered my prayers the night we met."

"You're kidding?" Cameron was unsure of what to make of this. "Why?"

"Because I felt the Spirit so strongly the night we met. And even though I knew I probably wouldn't see you again, I wanted to make sure that you had another chance to hear the gospel. I got the strongest feeling that night that you needed to hear more about our church," Lauren said.

"Your version of what happened sounds pretty noble. All I knew was I wanted to see you again—Mormon or not," Cameron said honestly.

Cameron turned Lauren's hand over in his, palm side up. He started to trace his index finger up and down each of her fingers. When he got to the band on her CTR ring, he flipped her hand over.

He gently pulled on her ring to remove it so he could look at it more closely. Lauren didn't stop him. She put her hand on his knee while he examined the ring.

Little silver animals, two-by-two, danced around the band. The CTR emblem was small but prominently displayed.

Lauren reached with her free hand into the pocket of her shorts. She pulled out his ring and said, "So why did you leave this at my house?"

Cameron shrugged his shoulders. "I'm not sure. I wanted you to know I had come by, and I don't exactly have calling cards."

"I thought you were so mad at me that you were getting rid of it. I thought it was a way of saying you were done with me and the Church."

"No, not at all. Well, at least not the 'you' part," Cameron said.

"So what about the Church? I mean, I don't want to get you all upset again, but can we talk some more about religion, or is that off limits?" Lauren asked.

Cameron exhaled audibly.

"That was a big sigh. Does that mean no?"

"No, not really. It's just . . . well, I guess it would be good if I could talk to someone about what's going on in my head. And maybe on some level I want to. The thing is, it's all mixed up right now. I'm not exactly sure if I can explain what I am feeling. Additionally, I don't want to pull you into all this." Cameron shook his head. "Now I sound like a girl."

"Hey! What's that supposed to mean?" Lauren said.

"Oh, you know. Girls are into drama and stuff. They always want to 'talk' things out."

"Maybe girls do that because it works. Boys are always keeping things in. They fuss and fume and hit each other when they get frustrated. Why don't we try the whole 'talk things out thing' and see if it works? I'll be your study buddy. If you get stuck, I'll give you a prompt."

Cameron eyed Lauren cautiously. "You're enjoying this, aren't you?"

"Immensely." Lauren smiled.

Cameron put Lauren's CTR ring back on her finger.

Lauren took Cameron's CTR ring and started to put it back on his finger. She kept her eyes on his, looking at him for a reaction. He didn't stop her.

Lauren whispered. "Cameron Thomas Richards, choose the right."

"I'm trying." He lowered his eyes. "But what is the right?"

"You have to find out for yourself. I mean, I can tell you what is right, at least what I know is right for me, but your 'right' may be different."

"You mean like the Mormon Church is right for you but may not be for me?"

"No. Actually, the Church is right for you too. You just may not know it yet."

"How can you say that? Don't you know everyone says that about their church?"

"Not everyone. Actually, there are only a few religions I know of that profess to be the 'right' church. The biggies are the Catholics, the Jews, and the Mormons. Other Protestant religions tend to think that believing in Christ is enough. My understanding is that to them it doesn't make much difference if you are Baptist, Methodist, or Assembly of God," Lauren said.

"That's basically true. That, in fact, is exactly how I was raised, but many of these groups take it a step further. If you are anything other than a mainstream Protestant religion, you are not just wrong, you are practically a devil worshiper. Do you learn about other religions in your church? I mean like in sermons and stuff?" Cameron asked.

"Never, well, almost never. I think I know what you are getting at, though. I went to a friend's church, and the lesson for the next week was listed on the bulletin board: The Cultist Religions: Seventh Day Adventists, Mormons, and Scientology. If you mean, do we do that, then no. At our church the focus is on Christ."

Cameron raised his eyebrows.

"Really," Lauren said. "We teach of Christ, we follow Christ, we remember Christ. We are a Christ-centered church."

"So where does Joseph Smith fit into all this?"

"He restored the gospel, but we don't worship him. We worship Christ."

Cameron leaned back in his seat, his head on the headrest. He wanted to believe the Mormon Church was, in fact, a Christian church, but another part of him fought it. He sat silent for a while.

Lauren allowed him his space for a few moments but then asked, "Is this where you need a prompt?" She put her hand on his arm.

"Oh, I don't know, it probably wouldn't be my first choice," Cameron said.

"I know what your first choice would be, not talking anymore, but I feel something here. I think we should go on. Do you feel it?"

"What?"

"The peace. The peace between us." Lauren smiled shyly at Cameron.

Was that what it was? Even though he didn't have all the answers—heck, he didn't even have all the questions—he had to admit that sitting here with Lauren, he was beginning to feel a kind of peace wash over him. He felt comfortable sitting next to her, and that comfort extended to their current conversation. He wasn't feeling a bit argumentative and, in fact, was surprised at how much sense she had made so far.

"Okay. What's your prompt?" Cameron asked.

"Well, answer me this. How do you see Christ? I mean, where does he fit in your life—and tell me what you think, not necessarily what other churches taught you."

"It's kind of hard to separate what I learned at church and what I think. I am not sure where one stops and the other starts, but my gut feeling is that he's my brother and he sacrificed his life for me, though I still marvel at that. I am not sure why he would do that. What was in it for him?"

"I think what was 'in it' was his ability to save his family whom he dearly loved. If we are his brothers and sisters and God is our Heavenly

Father, then it only makes sense that he would want to help us," Lauren said.

"I don't know. I don't think I would give my life for too many people—let alone the world."

"Granted, but we don't have the vision he did. We are Heavenly Father's children, but Christ was his firstborn. He understood from the beginning what his mission was. I think most of us struggle with that daily," Lauren said.

"Amen to that. I wish I knew what *my* mission was. I don't exactly understand why I'm here. I don't know where I'm supposed to go or what I'm supposed to do." Cameron paused and looked directly into Lauren's eyes. "I don't even know who the heck I am. I'm really struggling with finding out I have this whole extended family."

"Who am I? Where did I come from? Why am I here? Where am I going?" Lauren said. "Pretty basic questions, with pretty basic answers, actually."

"Right," Cameron said sarcastically.

"No, really. Take for example, 'Who am I?' You, Cameron T. Richards, are a child of God. You lived with him before you were born. He has known and loved you since the beginning of time."

Cameron involuntarily shivered.

Lauren continued. "You were created in his image. He then created this world for you to learn and grow in so you could become more like him. Eventually, you can return to live with him."

"Okay. I've heard most of that before—well, maybe not the 'lived with him before' part—but I see some sense in that. So why am I here? I mean me."

"Well, you are not here because of some cosmic accident. You are here to receive a body and to learn."

"Learn what?" Cameron asked.

"Oh, everything, I suppose. We're here to learn patience and love and mercy. We're here to learn things of the world and things of our Heavenly Father. We are here to learn algebra and to not fight with our families."

"Your church teaches you algebra?"

"No, silly. I just meant we are here to learn everything. Everything we learn here we take with us when we leave."

"Which brings us to 'where am I going?'"

"Yes, it does. So you already believe that death is not the end, right?"

"Right."

"Okay. Mormons believe that death is really just another beginning. It is another step forward. Our physical bodies die but not our spirits. Your spirit will never die, so at the time of your physical death, your spirit will go to the spirit world, and you will continue to learn and progress."

"More algebra?" Cameron said with a smile.

"Oh, probably calculus too." Lauren laughed.

"Well, I'm going to need an eternity for that one."

"Exactly, and Heavenly Father is offering us an eternity to continue to grow. But seriously, if you think about it, death is a necessary step in our progression, just like birth. Sometime after your death, your spirit and your body will be reunited. You believe in resurrection, don't you?"

"Yeah. 'Christ died that all men may live,' or something like that. I am not too good at quoting scripture."

"Sounds right to me."

"So go back to the 'lived with him before' part," Cameron said.

"Okay. Mormons believe that you didn't just spring into existence the moment you were born. You lived with your Heavenly Father."

"Where?"

"Oh, heaven, I suppose. I mean, I don't have the exact address, but I do know that we were with him before we came to earth."

"And?"

"And he knew that we needed more in order to progress. We needed a body, for example."

"Mormons believe you don't have bodies in heaven?" Cameron asked, somewhat shocked.

"Well, not in the premortal life. We were spirit children. That's part of the reason it was so important to come down here. We needed a body in order to really learn. We also needed to be away from him so we could learn on our own."

"Wouldn't it have been easier if he had just told us all this in heaven? I mean, why come to earth at all? Couldn't we have just skipped this whole part and stayed in heaven?"

"Not really. We didn't have bodies. That is something we had to come to earth to get. Plus, most people need to experience life, not just be told about it. How well do you learn if someone just tells you something? Don't you learn better when you do it yourself?"

"Eventually. But usually I mess up pretty bad before I get it," Cameron stated honestly.

"Right. Which brings us back to Christ. Heavenly Father knew we would mess up too. So he sent his son to atone for our mess-ups."

"Okay, I do believe that." Cameron sighed and closed his eyes.

"Big sigh again."

"Umm."

"You tired of talking? Do you want to go now?" Lauren asked.

"No." Cameron paused to try and figure out what he did want. "I want to sit here for a while."

"Do you want me to shut up?"

"Well, I don't think I would have said shut up, but maybe I could use a few moments of quiet while I process what you've told me."

"Sure." Lauren repositioned herself in the seat of the Jeep and sat motionless.

Finally, Cameron spoke. "Do you want to go for a walk?"

"Uh, sure. Where to?"

"I don't know. I just want to walk for a bit." Cameron jumped out of the Jeep onto the dried grasses that lined the side of the receding lake. He came around to Lauren's side and put his hand out to her. She took his left hand and jumped down. Cameron didn't let go of her hand after she was safely on the ground. Lauren didn't break the connection either.

Lauren and Cameron walked for a full fifteen minutes without a word between them, the soft underbelly of the forest gently crackling under their feet. Over rock and rill, they kept their hands locked. They were probably about a half-mile from the Jeep when Cameron spoke again. "Lauren, how can you be so sure of what you believe?"

"Because the Spirit witnessed to me. Look, Cameron, I haven't always believed it."

"I thought you were a Mormon your whole life," Cameron said with surprise.

"I have been, but even if you are born into the Church you have to find out for yourself. You can only rely on your parents' testimony for so long. At some point you have to find out for yourself or you will never stay in the Church. It's just too hard of a church to casually belong to."

"So how and when did you know?" Cameron had slowed to a stop and turned to face her.

"Probably my junior year in high school. I mean, that's when everything really settled in for me. I had an awesome seminary teacher that year, and we were reading the Book of Mormon, and . . ."

"What's seminary?"

"Oh, religion classes. They're held in the morning before school starts."

"You're not kidding this would be a hard church to belong to. You go to church almost seven days a week."

Lauren looked puzzled for a moment. "Oh! No, the classes are only for kids in high school. Sorry. I know I keep confusing you. Seminary is for high school students only, not the whole family. It's just an hour before school. So for me I went from 6:30 to 7:30."

"In the morning?"

"Of course in the morning. That's typically the time of day school starts," Lauren said teasingly. "School started at 7:45."

"So you are saying that you got up and went to your church for religious lessons every day before school?" Cameron couldn't decide if he was impressed with her dedication or if he wanted to run screaming from the forest because she was so fanatical.

"Basically."

"Wow. Did you do it on your own or did your parents make you go?"

"A little of both, I guess. In the beginning my parents made sure I went. I mean, they didn't really have to force me. It was okay to go. All my friends were there, but by the time I was a junior I suppose I could have rebelled and not gone. Some of my friends stopped going. But like I said, my junior year I got this really awesome teacher who really made me want to find out if the Church was true."

"So how did you find out?" Cameron asked.

"I think the biggest thing for me was actually reading the Book of Mormon. You see, our whole religion is really based on the Book of Mormon. If the Book of Mormon is true, then Joseph Smith really was a prophet and then everything else just falls into place. It all really does hinge on knowing if the Book of Mormon is true."

"So you read the book and . . . and what? What happened then?"

"Well, for me it was really just a confirmation of everything I had been taught. I didn't have any angels come down or burning bushes talk to me. I just read it, and every time I did I got the sweetest feelings of . . . well, truth, I suppose. I just began to know in my heart that it was true. Now pretty much everything I do is based on my testimony of the Book of Mormon."

"Even going out with me?"

"Especially going out with you. I know I am supposed to be with you right now. This may sound crazy to you, but for some reason I think I am the key to your lock."

Cameron blushed. "Or the key to my heart?"

"More like your soul. I think I am being asked to be your guide for the time being, and the reason I can be so sure of this is because I stay close to Heavenly Father by reading the Book of Mormon."

"I thought you said you had read it already," Cameron said.

"Oh, I did. But it's the kind of book you don't just read once and put on the shelf. You read it over and over. I'm probably on my third reading."

"I can't imagine reading a book three times. I mean, I read Harry Potter twice, but . . ."

"Listen, you read the Bible don't you? I mean, if you think about it, you have probably read some parts of it more than a dozen times. I mean, haven't you read the Christmas and Easter stories every year of your life?"

"Well, when you put it that way, yes. But I haven't read the Bible cover-to-cover."

"Not many people have. I had the Old Testament my freshman year in seminary. I don't think I actually read the whole thing. I'd like to, I mean, it's one of my goals, but for now I am content to read the Book of Mormon daily."

"You read the Book of Mormon every day?"

"Just about."

"So today, you read the Book of Mormon today?"

"Well, yes. I read this morning."

"Lauren, there is no way I could . . ." Cameron's voice trailed off. Cameron had thought from the beginning that Lauren was like an angel, but now he realized that she was more spiritual than he could ever hope to be. He lowered his head in sadness, realizing that he could never actually be with her.

"What?" Lauren whispered.

Cameron let go of her hand, shook his head, and avoided her eyes.

"What, Cameron? You can talk to me, really."

"It's just, well, I thought that maybe you . . . oh, I don't know. I thought that you coming over tonight was because . . . but now, well, maybe I misread something."

"Cameron, you aren't making any sense. What did you think? Let me help you." Lauren reached out and took both of his hands in hers.

Cameron didn't want her help, he didn't want her to take his hands, but he was weak and didn't pull away. He loved her touch, even though it brought him more pain. Then Lauren did something that changed everything. She let go of his hands, put both of them on his cheeks, and pulled him down to her. She kissed him gently and full on the lips. It was the sweetest, most pure kiss he had ever had. It was given freely and without reservation.

Cameron wrapped his arms around Lauren in a hold so tight that he was afraid he might break her in two. He buried his head in the crook of her neck, which may have been a mistake because he could smell the sweetness of her lingering perfume mingled with the scent of her shampoo, or conditioner—he didn't know which. It didn't matter. She smelled like an angel, she looked like an angel, she definitely kissed like an angel, and she was standing here with him, her arms gently wrapped around his neck.

He finally got up the courage to whisper in her ear, "Lauren, you are the single most confusing person I have ever met."

"Is that bad?" she whispered back in his ear. Her soft breath tickled, and he shivered in response.

"No, it's good. All good. But I am confused. What do you want?

Why do you preach to me one minute and then kiss me the next? What kind of conversion plan is this?"

"I don't know. I think I am making it up as I go along," she answered honestly.

"What do you want me to do?"

"Really?"

"Yes, really. What do you want me to do?"

"Read the Book of Mormon."

"And?" Cameron asked. He knew there had to be more.

"That's it. Just read the Book of Mormon. Everything else will just fall in place. I feel it in my heart."

"You don't want me to go to your church?"

"Well, sure, I'd love for you to come to church, but church is not the important thing."

"How can you say that?" Cameron loosened his grip on her and pulled back a bit to look her in the eyes. "What church wouldn't think that going to church was the most important thing?"

"Look, just read the Book of Mormon. I promise, everything else will fall in place. You could go to church for years and not believe the Church is true. But you only have to read the Book of Mormon once to gain a testimony of it and then you would want to go to church."

"Well, I'll read it, then, if it's that important to you."

"Cameron, it is way more important for you than it is for me. I've already read it."

"I know, three times," Cameron teased.

Just then the shrill beeping of a cell phone interrupted their conversation. Lauren's pocket was ringing.

She fished the cell phone out of her pocket and pushed "talk."

"Hello? . . . Out at the lake . . . I know, I'm coming home soon . . . No . . . Yes . . . No, that's just the phone, I'm not getting a good signal . . . Okay, I will . . . Love you too." Lauren clicked the "end" button.

"Your mom?" Cameron asked

"None else. She likes keeping tabs on me, but I do have to go home sometime soon. Do you think we could start walking back to your Jeep?"

"Of course," Cameron said as he reached down and took her hand again.

"It's a pretty night tonight, isn't it?"

"Beautiful," Cameron answered simply, but in his mind he was thinking it was the most glorious night he had ever had. He still couldn't believe she had kissed him. He figured it was probably a good thing she had, though, because he didn't know if he would have ever mustered the courage to kiss her. She was too good, too perfect, for him to have ever guessed that she would be with him.

"Cameron?"

"Umm?"

"When do you think you will read the Book of Mormon?"

"Well, I suppose I would start tonight if I had one. Where do I get one?"

"Really? Tonight? You would read the Book of Mormon tonight?"

"Yes. That's what I said. If I had a Book of Mormon, I would read it—starting tonight."

"Well, not to be pushy, but I can get you one as soon as we get home."

"Pushy? Now Lauren, who would ever think you were pushy?"

"You're teasing me now, right?" Lauren asked.

"Right."

"Okay, just so we don't argue again. I hate it when we argue."

"Me too," Cameron said honestly, although the whole make-up thing had turned out better than he would have ever dared to hope.

"Cameron?" Lauren said, her voice quiet with meaning.

Cameron stopped walking, and Lauren stood looking at him.

"What?"

"Well, I just want you to know that none of this was planned. I mean, you probably think I'm really forward now. I know you said you were teasing about the 'pushy' part, but I know I am. I mean, I know I can be."

"Look, Lauren, if you weren't outspoken, we would never be here tonight. If you hadn't given me grief at the restaurant, I wouldn't be walking here with you now. I know I tease you, but I really do like that you speak your mind and that you're so sure of things."

"Really?"

In answer Cameron leaned forward and kissed her—not a

tentative, surprise kiss, but a boy-kiss, full of warmth and meaning. A kiss of beginnings and a kiss of acceptance. All and all, the best kiss of his life.

When Cameron walked into his grandmother's house, it was after eleven o'clock. He needed to get to bed, but he had promised Lauren he would read her Book of Mormon.

When Lauren had said she would get him one, he didn't know she was going to give him hers. He had told her he could wait until he got one of his own, but she insisted, saying they had a dozen or more copies of it at her house, which, frankly, he found to be unbelievable.

When she brought it out, it was in a blue-flowered cloth cover. She took the cover off to reveal a well-worn, navy, leather book of scriptures. She called it a quad. She made bookmarks by tearing little pieces of paper from a pizza advertisement that she had taken from a pile of junk mail next to the family's kitchen phone. She showed him where the Book of Mormon started and finished, because there were other scriptures in the book as well. A lot of the pages were marked in red pencil. You could tell that this was a daily driver; it wasn't kept in a garage for good looks.

She said she thought that the missionaries suggested you start with Third Nephi and marked that, but really as long as he was reading it, it didn't matter to her if he started there or at the beginning. She was overly excited and reminded him of a three-year-old as she was trying to explain things to him all at once. She would start one sentence, stop, and then go somewhere completely different with her train of thought. More than once he had put his fingers on her lips to stop her mid-sentence so she could finish one thought at a time.

He met Lauren's mother briefly when she came in to get a drink of water in the kitchen. She didn't stay long enough for him to really form an impression.

Now back in the quiet of his own room, he opened the book.

He kind of flipped through the pages Lauren had bookmarked. It read sort of like the New Testament. The English was similar, but it was a little easier to understand.

One passage that Lauren had insisted he read first was Moroni 10:4. In Lauren's handwriting "Moroni's promise" was written in the side margin. She had underlined verses 3 through 5, so that is what he read.

"Behold, I would exhort you that when ye shall read these things, if it be wisdom in God that ye should read them, that ye would remember how merciful the Lord hath been unto the children of men, from the creation of Adam even down until the time that ye shall receive these things, and ponder it in your hearts.

"And when ye shall receive these things, I would exhort you that ye would ask God, the Eternal Father, in the name of Christ, if these things are not true; and if ye shall ask with a sincere heart, with real intent, having faith in Christ, he will manifest the truth of it unto you, by the power of the Holy Ghost. And by the power of the Holy Ghost ye may know the truth of all things."

Cameron reread the passage three times. He thought it was kind of bold for this person to ask people to "ask God" if this book was true. Whoever wrote this must have been feeling pretty confident at the time.

Well, he didn't think that you could tell if a book was "true" after reading three verses, but he did need to know if what he was doing was okay with his Heavenly Father. And he did know how to pray, so he got on his knees next to his bed and asked for wisdom.

It was a simple prayer, with a simple, clear answer. He crawled into his bed and opened the book.

The book actually opened to a section in Third Nephi. Lauren had marked this part, so he figured this was as good a place as any to start. He read chapter 10 and set the book on his chest. His heart was pounding. He picked up the book and reread chapter 10. It appeared to be the voice of Christ speaking to a group of people who had recently undergone some type of great calamity. There were over four references to gathering his people as a hen gathered her chickens. He wasn't quite sure what that meant, but it seemed to speak to some part of him.

The other verse that caught him off guard was when the author of this book seemed to be speaking right to him in verse 14. The scripture said, "And now, whoso readeth, let him understand; he that hath the scriptures, let him search them." To Cameron the scripture said, "And now, Cameron, if you're reading this, try to understand; if you have scriptures, search them."

He set the book down again on his chest. Then he closed the book so he didn't have to look at it. In a moment he picked up the book again and opened it to read more.

If he thought chapter 10 was unsettling, chapter 11 blew him away. His hands begin to tremble as he read of Christ descending out of heaven. As he finished the chapter, his breath was coming in short, quick puffs. He stretched his arms out in front of him and watched as his fingers danced and shook at the end of his hands. What did this mean?

He took a deliberate, deep breath—and then another. He flipped to the first pizza bookmark. He wanted to start at the beginning.

He read the introduction and "The Testimony of Three Witnesses." Surprisingly, everything he read seemed pretty straightforward.

He read the "Testimony of the Prophet Joseph Smith" twice. Could this possibly be true? On the surface the story seemed fantastic, but his heart told him that what he was reading was true. He wanted to call Lauren and talk to her—right now. He looked at his watch. It was past midnight, and he had to work in the morning.

He closed the book and set it on his nightstand. He turned the light out.

He lay on his back for a while; then he turned to the right and tried curling up with his pillow. He put the pillow over his head. He kicked the sheets off. He turned to the left. He told his brain to go to sleep. He hit the light button on his watch. Fifteen minutes had gone by. He said a silent prayer. He prayed for sleep, but his body wouldn't comply.

At 1 A.M. he gave in to his curiosity. He turned the light back on and opened the Book of Mormon to First Nephi and began to read.

WEDNESDAY

"Cameron, you don't look like you slept very well. How do you feel?" his grandmother asked with concern when he lumbered into the kitchen. It was 6:30 A.M. and, frankly, Cameron was surprised he had woken up at all. He thought he had gotten all of two hours of sleep.

"No. I didn't get much sleep, but I'm a big boy and I'll be okay. I'll just go to bed early tonight."

"When did you get home? Did Zach's truck take longer than you thought it would?"

Cameron laughed a short snort of a laugh. Zach's truck was ancient history. It was before Lauren kissed him, before he kissed Lauren, before he read about one-third of the book Lauren had given him. It seemed days ago that he had been under Zach's truck. "No. I got done with Zach's truck pretty quickly, actually. Then I went to the lake with a friend, and we talked for a while."

His grandmother's eyebrows arched a bit when he said "friend," but she didn't question him.

She had a lunch set out for him on the counter. Two eggs, sunny-side up, were on the table. He was especially grateful for her help this morning. He set his wadded up jean jacket on the table and proceeded to eat his eggs.

"Oh, I don't think you're going to need a coat today. It's supposed to be in the high 90s."

Cameron looked at his coat. He had wrapped Lauren's book inside so he wouldn't have to explain anything to his grandmother. He planned on reading more at lunch.

"Oh, I know it's going to be hot. It's just," Cameron quickly lied, "I normally keep this jacket in my Jeep. I accidentally brought it in."

"I see. Oh, I almost forgot." His grandmother walked into the living room as she continued talking. "I was going to give this to you last night but, well, you came home so late." She walked back into the room with a large, old shoebox, or maybe it was a boot box, Cameron wasn't sure. "I figured you might want to see this." She set the box on the table in front of him and stood waiting for him to open it.

He pulled the lid off and peered inside at remnants of his father's life. Cameron pulled out an olive green sash with merit badges on it. Some of the merit badges he recognized because he had been in Scouting too. There were pictures and small trophies lying on their side. There were two black books of scripture neatly stacked one on top of the other. One was clearly the Bible, the other was a combination of the Book of Mormon, the Doctrine and Covenants, and the Pearl of Great Price. He gently lifted the Book of Mormon out.

To the amazement of his grandmother, he ran his hands reverently down the side of the pages, pages that had clearly not been opened, pages that ink and time had fused together. The book had never been used.

"Those were your dad's seminary scriptures, but he never went much," his grandmother offered in way of explanation.

Obviously, Cameron thought but didn't voice. What he did say was, "Early morning seminary?"

"Yes. How did you know about that?" she asked with surprise in her voice.

"Oh, Lauren told me about it last night," Cameron said casually, but in his current state of sleep deprivation, it came out with a yawn.

"Lauren? Stacy's friend?"

"Uh-huh. I was sort of asking her questions about the Mormon Church."

"Oh," was all his grandmother said.

Cameron swallowed the last bite of egg and said, "I've got to run. Thanks for breakfast," and as he picked up his brown paper sack, he added, "and lunch."

Much to his amazement, by ten o'clock he was running on all his boy cylinders. It probably had something to do with the two caffeine-filled colas he had bought on the way into work, but he was managing okay. No one at work mentioned his tired, bloodshot eyes.

Lunch found him sitting in his car, which he had moved out of the full sun and into the shade of a large nearby oak tree. He had finished his lunch and was reading from the Book of Mormon again.

He was so absorbed in what he was reading that he didn't see Rock until he was next to his Jeep.

"Hi, ya," Rock said as he glanced at the book of scriptures Cameron was holding.

"Oh, hi. I didn't even hear you come up."

"Yeah, I could see you were pretty focused. You reading the Bible?" Rock asked.

"Uh, no. Actually, it's the Book of Mormon."

"What?" Rock's voice was instantly edged with annoyance. "You never said you were Mormon." He almost spit the words out.

Cameron was a little surprised at Rock's reaction, even though he knew it was the exact reaction he had had upon finding out all his relatives were Mormon. "I'm not Mormon," Cameron said evenly.

"Then why are you reading that trash?" Rock asked.

"Well, it turns out my whole family is. I told you I came here to stay with my dad's relatives, relatives I didn't really know I had. They're all Mormon."

"Bummer."

Cameron at first didn't know how to respond to that. He didn't think his family was so bad. They were turning out to be the nicest, kindest people he had ever met, though he didn't say that to Rock. Instead he replied, "Yeah, a little."

"So are they forcing you to read this crap? Why would you go along with it?" Rock asked.

"No, they aren't forcing me. In fact, they don't even know I'm reading it. I got the book from this girl I met, and I figured I should read it to see what makes Mormons tick." Cameron smiled. He thought that was a pretty good explanation.

"Oh, I know what makes them tick all right—Satan." Rock said it with absolute finality.

"Well, maybe. That's what I've always thought too. But this book seems pretty harmless. There are a lot of references to Christ in it," Cameron said.

"Their way of perverting the truth. I think you're crazy for even holding it. The book is 100 percent devil worship." Rock shook his head disgustedly.

"How can you say that? Have you read it?" Cameron was getting irritated now and his voice showed it.

"I've read enough to know to stay away from it. Why are you defending it?"

"I'm not defending it. I'm reading it." Cameron said.

"Sounds like you're being sucked into something you don't know nothin' about," Rock said.

"Look, man, I'm just reading the book. I'm not joining their church." Cameron was getting angrier by the minute that he was having to defend his reading of the Book of Mormon.

"Okay, okay, read the stupid book, but when they get their claws on you, don't come whining to me." Rock turned around and stomped back to the shop.

Cameron turned back to where he had been, but the angry confrontation with Rock had left him unsettled. He sighed and yawned at the same time. He closed the book.

What he really wanted was a nap and to talk to Lauren. He wished he could call her, but even that was impossible. He didn't have her phone number. Heck, he hadn't even known her last name until last night when she had handed him the book the first time. It was printed on the front cover: Lauren Emma Smith.

He sat for a while just holding the book, her book. It made him feel close to her. He leaned his head back on the seat. He closed his eyes and could see faint images of Lauren. He could feel her touching him. He could smell her. He could hear her.

"Cameron?"

Cameron opened his eyes with a start. Someone was gently shaking his arm. He jerked involuntarily to a full, upright position.

"I think you fell asleep," Lauren said simply.

"What the . . . ? Where'd you come from? How'd you know where I worked?" His tired brain was fuzzy with questions.

"I got your grandmother's number from Stacy, and she told me you worked here. I figured I'd be safe if I came down around noon. Don't most people take lunch around noon? I didn't mean to bother you, though. I mean, I probably shouldn't have woken you up. By the way, you don't look so good. It's probably my fault, right? Did I keep you up too late? I'm really sorry."

Lauren did have a gift for chattering on, Cameron thought, but right now it was music to his ears. She had a habit of asking questions in succession that he didn't think she really wanted answers for. When she was nervous, he discovered, she seemed to talk for talking's sake.

"Lauren," he finally broke in, "pick a question, any question, and I'll answer it."

Lauren stopped talking and looked at him, slightly offended and partly embarrassed.

"Ah, don't look at me like that. I didn't mean to hurt your feelings. I'm just tired, and you're asking too many questions at once. Just pick one." Cameron yawned.

"Well," Lauren started tentatively, "did you have a chance to read any of the book?"

Cameron looked at the book on his lap. Surely she could see it too.

Lauren also looked at the book in his lap and waited for an answer.

"Yes, as a matter of fact, I did, though that wasn't one of your original questions."

"No, but only because you stopped me before I got to it. It was, however, one of the most important questions. I just couldn't wait. I'm terribly impatient sometimes."

"I'm about a third of the way through the book."

Lauren's eyes opened to their widest point and then began to tear up.

"Hey, you're not crying are you?" Cameron gently demanded.

"A little," Lauren whispered.

"Why?"

"I just knew it. I knew in my heart you would read it, but even I didn't know you would *read* read it."

"What?"

Lauren shook her head. "Well, I hoped you would read it, but I would have been grateful if you had only read one verse on one page. I never expected you to actually read the book."

"You asked me to read the book, right? So, I'm reading it."

"But Cameron, this is such a big deal. I mean you're *reading* it," Lauren said.

"Stop. You're giving me a headache."

"So what do you think?" Lauren asked.

"Well, it's different. It's not too hard to read and . . ." his voice trailed off.

"What? Tell me everything," Lauren said.

Cameron shook his head.

"Please," Lauren pleaded.

"Lauren, the truth is, I'm tired. I stayed up until 4:30 reading this book. I don't want to say anything yet because I am still trying to decipher what I'm feeling. I don't know where my feelings for you stop and start. I am afraid that the 'us' may be influencing how I'm feeling about this book."

"So you're feeling good?"

"Yes, but that may just be because of how I feel toward you right now."

"No. No, it's not. It's the book. It's not me."

"Lauren, you don't know that. You don't know how I feel."

"But I do. I was there last night too. If you are feeling positive when you read the book, it's all the book, not me. I could walk away today, and you would still feel good about the book. I'm sure of it."

"Whoa. I don't think so, and please don't try it," Cameron said.

"So, do you have any questions?" Lauren asked.

"Tons."

"I know I'm pushy, but do you want to maybe get together again and talk?"

"Lauren Emma Smith, are you asking me out—again?"

"How'd you know my . . ."

Cameron pointed to the name embossed on her scriptures.

"Oh," Lauren said simply.

"So?"

"I don't think it would be like a date exactly since no food would be involved, so technically, I'm not asking you out." Lauren smiled at her logic.

"What's wrong with asking me out?" Cameron continued.

"Oh, I just don't think girls should ask guys out."

"Why not?"

"Not proper, I suppose, and besides, I don't get paid till Friday, so what kind of a date could I take you on?"

"I thought last night was good."

Lauren smiled. "It was, wasn't it?"

"Umm." Cameron smiled at the memory.

"When do you have to be back at work?"

Cameron glanced at his watch and practically jumped right over Lauren trying to get out of his Jeep. "Five minutes ago. I can't believe I'm late from lunch my second day."

"Well, what about tonight?" Lauren walked rapidly behind him. "Do you want to get together?"

"Of course."

"Well, do you want to call me?" Lauren asked.

Cameron stopped for a second in the parking lot and turned to face her. "I don't have your number."

"It's in the front of my scriptures. Look on the inside cover. You can just call me at home. I'll be waiting."

"Okay, I get off at four. I'll call you when I get home."

Lauren smiled and her face lit up.

Cameron kissed his finger and touched her lips. "See you later then."

The black vinyl seats of Cameron's Jeep seared through his jeans as he got in at 4 P.M. The heat outside was still and suffocating. This was the first day that the weather in the Sacramento Valley had really bothered him. His Jeep didn't have air-conditioning, of course, and the flow of air he kicked up as he drove toward his grandmother's brought no relief. It was super-highway-heated air that made images in front of him ripple in miniature, vibrating waves. He was tired, hungry, and thirsty. He needed sleep, and he needed to talk to Lauren—he didn't know which one was going to win. He knew he had told her he would see her tonight, but he was just so overcome with fatigue that all he wanted to do was sleep.

He only took the slightest notice that someone had parked in his usual spot across from his grandmother's house. He pulled a U-turn and parked right in front of the house. His sweaty jeans stuck slightly to the seat as he got out. He thought he probably was going to need shorts of some kind. He didn't own any—he hadn't really needed any in Fargo.

He opened the door and was grateful for the wave of cool, air-conditioned air that enveloped him. He could hear muffled voices coming from the back of the house—girl voices. Then he heard his grandmother's voice. They must be in her bedroom. He kicked off his shoes at the front door and walked toward his bedroom. The door to his grandmother's room was closed. He was more tired than curious. He didn't bother to knock; he was going to take a nap. She would figure out soon enough, by the shoes at the door, that he was home. His need for sleep was winning out. He would call Lauren in a bit.

His bedroom door was open, and the first thing he noticed was a wrapped package on his pillow. Bright ribbons fell playfully across his pillowcase. He blinked twice trying to focus on the present. At first he viewed it as only one more impediment to sleep. He didn't have the cognitive skills to process why there was something on his bed. He wanted to throw himself on his sheets and crash, but even in his half-dazed condition, he knew he was going to have to shower first—employment in the automotive industry meant dirty, greasy work.

He grabbed a pair of boxers and his clean khakis and headed for the bathroom.

He was still tired, but the cool rivulets of water felt wonderful on his face. He lowered his head and closed his eyes. He let the water pour over him. There was a small, tentative knock at the door.

"Cameron?" the muffled voice of his grandmother asked.

"Yeah?" He raised his voice over the sound of the water.

"You have company," she said.

"What?" He must not have heard her right. He shook his head to get the water out of his ears.

"What'd you say, Gramma?"

"I . . . said . . . you . . . have . . . com . . . pa . . . ny." She separated each syllable with a short pause.

Cameron's eyebrows furrowed a bit. Who would come and visit him? His brain was working overtime. "Okay, Gramma, I'll be right out," he finally replied.

He yawned again and stretched. He reluctantly turned off the water.

He hadn't brought a shirt into the bathroom with him, so he hoped his company was not female. He dressed and towel dried his hair but didn't comb it. It fell recklessly over his forehead, tightly curled from the shower. He cracked the door to peek out. He could see into his room. Sitting on his bed was his cousin Stacy. Lauren was standing with her back to him. Well, so much for modesty. He opened the door and walked toward his room.

"Hi, Cameron," Stacy said. "I hope you don't mind that I brought Lauren in here. I wanted to show her what we did with your dad's old room."

"No, it's okay," Cameron lied as he walked toward his dresser. He actually did feel a little odd with them both in his room while he was half-naked. He could feel Lauren's eyes on him and he shivered.

"I had to come over because Aunt Clara is letting me borrow one of her old dresses for a skit I'm supposed to be in at church."

"Oh," he said, with his back to them both. He pulled out a clean, white T-shirt and tugged it over his head and shoulders.

"Lauren just came along for the ride," Stacy added.

Cameron smiled indulgently.

"You seem kind of quiet," Stacy said, fishing for more conversation.

"Just tired. Long day at work." Cameron was not going to bite.

"Oh, well, maybe we'd better go then."

Shoot, plot complication, he thought. He wanted Stacy to leave but not Lauren, who still had not said so much as "hello" to him. She had nodded when he walked in, but other than that she was verbally silent. Now he could feel her all over his bedroom, and it made him crazy.

"No. I'm sorry. I didn't mean to be rude. I'm just surprised to see you both. You're my first visitors since I've arrived. How long can you stay?" He leaned up against the wall as he spoke.

"Well, Aunt Clara actually asked us to stay for dinner. I hadn't really said if we could or not yet."

"Please do. I'm hungry, and all things considered, I do feel much better now that I've showered. I think my being so tired is just a combination of not getting much sleep the past couple of nights and the heat out here."

"Lauren needs to call her mom," Stacy said.

"There's a phone in the kitchen," Cameron offered.

Lauren spoke for the first time. "I have my cell phone." She reached into her purse and fished it out to show them.

"I think I want one of those," Cameron said. "Well, maybe I need friends first."

"Sometimes it's a pain when your mom calls so often," Lauren said.

"How often does she call you?" Cameron asked.

"At least a million times a day." Lauren shook her head in annoyance.

"A million? How can you afford it?" Cameron teased. At that moment Lauren's phone began ringing.

Lauren looked at the number of the incoming call and rolled her eyes. "Guess I don't have to call my mom now." She hit the button on her phone. "Hello, Mom . . . Over at Stacy's great-aunt's in Roseville . . . No, they invited me for dinner. I was just about to call. No, Mom, really." Lauren shook her head and rolled her eyes even bigger.

Cameron smiled.

"Of course, Mom . . . I'll call later . . . Yeah . . . Bye." Lauren ended the call and put the phone back in her purse. She smiled. "I can stay."

"Okay, then," Cameron sighed in relief. "When is dinner?"

"Aunt Clara said anytime we want. She said she had salads and cold cuts because it's so hot out."

"Oh my heck, that sounds good," Cameron said. Then Cameron laughed. "I can't believe I just said that."

"Said what?" Stacy asked.

"Said, 'Oh my heck.'"

"Why, what's wrong with it?" Lauren asked.

"Nothing, other than it's weird. But the thing is, Zach kept saying it yesterday when we were working on his car. I thought it was a peculiar saying is all—and now I'm using it."

"Oh, well, we hear it all the time. It's sort of a Utah thing," Stacy said.

"What do you mean?"

Stacy continued. "I mean people in Utah seem to use it a lot. Zach has a lot of Utah relatives. He's the person around here who says it most. Well, I take that back. Everyone who comes home from the Y uses it too."

"The Y?"

"BYU. Brigham Young University," Lauren clarified and then added, "I'm going there in a few weeks. I'm sure I told you."

Cameron had to think back to all the conversations he had had with Lauren. He vaguely remembered her saying she was going away to school, but at the time it was fairly meaningless to him. Now it took on new significance.

"Right, your brother is going on a mission or something, and you're going off to school. You're both leaving at the same time," Cameron recited.

"Very good," Lauren smiled.

Cameron turned to Stacy. "What about you? Are you going to BYU?"

"I don't know yet. I may. I'll probably do another semester at Sierra. My grades aren't as good as Lauren's. I may be able to transfer in if I do well this term. How about you Cameron? Have you been to college?" Stacy asked.

"Me? No. I did mostly vocational stuff in high school. My grades were okay, but going to college was not in the picture financially. I wanted to get out of the house as soon as I could, so I went the auto class route."

"Does that mean you would have gone if the money hadn't been an issue?" Lauren asked.

"Possibly, but it doesn't seem likely now. I have to support myself."

"Well, there are scholarships," Lauren said.

"I did okay in high school, but most of the kids who were getting scholarships were more active in other stuff besides school. Probably the only reason I have a 3.9 GPA is because of all the auto classes I aced."

"You have a 3.9 GPA?" Stacy said in clear astonishment.

"Yeah, but it's no big deal. There was nothing much else to do where I grew up. I studied."

"So why not a 4.0?" Lauren asked.

"Oh, actually because I got an F my sophomore year, and I never retook the class."

"What class?"

"Communication studies," Cameron said evenly. At this revelation Lauren started to laugh. She actually had to grab at her sides and bend over to catch her breath. Stacy and Cameron both just stared at her.

"Why is that so funny, Lauren?" Stacy asked.

"Inside joke," Lauren choked out.

Cameron wasn't laughing.

"I'm hungry. You girls don't mind if we go eat now, do you?" He turned his back to Lauren and Stacy and started to leave the room.

"Hey, wait," Stacy said. "You never opened the present Lauren brought you. Didn't you see it?"

Cameron had forgotten all about the gift on his pillow. He had planned on looking at it after he got out of the shower, but then everything got all mixed up with the girls being in his room.

"Oh, sure." He walked back in the room. He reached behind Lauren, who had sat down on his bed. She was quiet and eyed him carefully as he took the package. It was heavier than he expected. He pulled off the wrappings to expose a box. He lifted the lid. Under white tissue wrapping was a leather book. Embossed in gold block letters in the lower right hand corner were two lines:

CAMERON THOMAS RICHARDS
CHOOSE THE RIGHT

Stacy gasped. "You bought him a quad?"

"Yes," Lauren answered simply.

Cameron ran his fingers over the name in the corner and looked at Lauren in puzzlement.

"You needed it," she said in answer to his questioning look.

"You bought him a quad," Stacy repeated. "Wow."

"Lauren, you didn't have to do this. This book must have cost you a lot of money, and I know you don't have much."

"I have a savings account and I wanted to," Lauren said.

"Lauren, no offense, but isn't a quad a little premature for Cameron? I mean, he's only been exposed to the Church for, what, three days?" Stacy said.

"Five, actually. Lauren told me a lot about it when I first met her on Saturday," Cameron responded to his cousin.

"Do you even know what a quad is?" Stacy asked, continuing to be baffled at Lauren's choice of gifts.

"Actually, I do. Lauren gave me hers."

"And he's read over a third of the Book of Mormon already," Lauren said.

"What?" Stacy's mouth opened and then closed.

Cameron and Lauren continued to lock eyes.

"Why?" Stacy finally muttered.

With this question, Lauren turned to Stacy. "Why does anyone read the Book of Mormon? Because they have questions. Cameron had questions, and I told him this was where he could find the answers."

"I know, but I just wouldn't have expected it," Stacy said.

"Why?" Cameron asked Stacy. "Because I don't fit the part?"

"Well, that, and . . ." She didn't finish her sentence.

"What? What else?" Cameron knew there was something more she was holding back.

"Well, the whole thing with your dad. I mean my dad said he was pretty anti-Mormon. I just wouldn't have expected you to have anything to do with the Church."

"Oh, that. Well, actually, he didn't talk much about the Church—I didn't even know he was a Mormon until three days ago. If I had anti-Mormon feelings, it was because of all the other Christian churches I went to."

Stacy turned to Lauren. "I still can't believe you gave him a quad. Why not just one of the missionary Books of Mormon?"

"Because," Lauren shrugged her shoulders, "he's worth more than a buck-fifty to me."

When Cameron had passed by the kitchen earlier, he hadn't even noticed that there were balloons and streamers hanging from the ceiling. He had been just too tired to consider anything else but sleep. Now he could see that on the table was a red, white, and blue birthday cake. He assumed that if he counted all the white candles they would add up to twenty-one.

He was equally touched and embarrassed by his grandmother's gesture.

The table was set with three white dinner plates and an old, chipped red one. His grandmother directed him to the seat in front of the festive, older plate.

"Cameron, this is the plate we use when someone has a birthday or some other special event," his grandmother said, touching the antique-looking plate.

"I think everyone in our family has eaten off that plate at one time or another," his cousin Stacy added.

"That's so special," Lauren said to Cameron's grandmother. "How old is the plate?"

"Oh, gosh, maybe sixty years old. My mother-in-law gave it to me when I first married Grandpa Richards."

Cameron reached for a white envelope tucked under his plate. It had his name written in neatly printed block letters. Everyone paused as he opened the envelope. Inside of a store-bought birthday card, Cameron counted out twenty-one crisp ten-dollar bills. He let out a little gasp. It was as much money as he had ever made in a week at the gas station in North Dakota.

"Wow, Gramma, this is really too much. I don't think I can accept it," Cameron said, holding the money out toward his grandmother.

His grandmother shooed the money away by waving her hand in the air in his direction. "Nonsense," she said. "Mike's kids have gotten ten dollars each year for their birthday since they were born. I've just been saving yours all these years. I should probably have added interest." His grandmother and the girls laughed in unison.

Cameron was still a bit embarrassed, but he lowered the money and put it back into the envelope. "Well, thank you. This really means a lot to me."

"You're welcome. Now let's eat."

Cameron realized he was really hungry now that he could see the food. He put three sandwiches and two different kinds of salads on his plate—although he had to pick the avocados out of one of them. What was with Californians and their avocados anyway?

He was just about to bite into a sandwich when he saw that the others were waiting for something. He quickly realized they wanted to pray.

After the prayer Stacy directed a question toward his grandmother. "Aunt Clara, did you know Cameron is reading the Book of Mormon?"

"No." Clara looked at Cameron for confirmation. "I didn't."

Cameron had to nod in acknowledgement, because his mouth was full. It annoyed him that Stacy had told his grandmother. He wasn't really ready to discuss this with her yet.

"He's read almost a third of it. I don't know where he finds the time," Stacy said as she bit into her sandwich. With a partially stuffed mouth, she added, "Good grief, he's only been here a couple of days. I haven't even gotten that far."

"Really, Cameron?" Grandma Clara asked.

Cameron swallowed hard. "Yeah, well, Lauren gave me the book last night and asked me to read it. So, well, I did."

"Last night? Is that why you were so tired this morning?"

"Yeah, kind of."

"Oh, Cameron." His grandmother turned away from him to wipe her eyes on the back of her hand and then stood and took her plate to the sink.

"Oh, Cameron," was all she said. Cameron was grateful she hadn't asked a bunch of questions he wasn't prepared to answer yet. Just tears and an "Oh, Cameron."

"Lauren, I have to leave pretty soon. I have to go over and practice this skit thing. Do you want to come or . . ." She let the question hang in the air.

Lauren looked at Cameron.

"I can take her home, if that's what you mean," he said to Stacy.

Lauren let a pent-up breath of air out and smiled.

"Okay, then, I'm off." Stacy stood and went to the sink to give her great-aunt a hug. "Thanks for dinner."

"You're welcome, sweetie. Anytime, you know that," Clara said.

"Lauren," Cameron said later as they were getting into his Jeep, "I feel a little awkward accepting this book from you." He held up his new quad that he had carried with him to the truck.

"I know," Lauren said as she buckled herself in.

"Just because I am reading it doesn't mean I believe it."

"I know," Lauren said again.

"Well, can you at least get your money back if it doesn't work out?" Cameron asked.

"No. I had it imprinted, but it doesn't matter. I wouldn't take it back anyway."

"But it must have cost a lot of money," Cameron said, thinking back to how astonished Stacy had been at the gift.

Lauren just looked at him for a moment before replying. "It did. But I look at it as an investment in the future."

Cameron caught her gaze and gently asked, "Whose? Yours or mine?"

Lauren didn't blink and leaned forward slightly. "Maybe both." She smiled.

Cameron leaned back away from her but held her eyes. Finally, he closed his eyes to break the connection and shook his head. When he opened them again, Lauren was looking at something lodged under her seat. She reached down and pulled out a pack of cigarettes. She held them up.

"Yours?" she asked.

Cameron shrugged. "Yeah." He felt a little uncomfortable with her holding his cigarettes. He remembered that they had fallen out of his glove box when he dropped the ring off at Lauren's. He had never gotten around to fishing them out from under the seat and now Lauren held them in her hands.

"I thought you quit a couple of months ago," she said, clearly referring to the fact that this was a fresh pack.

"I did."

Lauren didn't say anything. Cameron knew she was waiting for an explanation. *How much do I really he owe her?* he thought stubbornly.

When Cameron didn't reply, Lauren handed the pack to him. He took it, leaned over her, unlatched the glove box, and threw it in.

"I'm not Mormon, Lauren," he said.

"I know," she said in a quiet voice.

"So I guess you want me to take you home, then?" he asked in response to her suddenly quiet demeanor. He took this to mean she was upset again.

"Not really," she said.

Cameron just looked at her for a moment. Surprise was written on the furrows of his forehead.

"Really? I thought . . ." His words trailed off as he glanced at the glove box.

"Just don't smoke around me, okay?"

"No. No, I won't," Cameron stammered. He was so astonished at her generosity—given that he knew how she felt about smoking—that he all of a sudden wanted to hold her close and tell her the whole stupid story of why the cigarettes were even there.

"Lauren, do you know anyplace cool that we could go?" Cameron's shirt was sticking to his back. He leaned forward and pulled the cotton-poly material away from his skin.

"Like the mall?"

"No. Someplace quiet, someplace where I can ask you questions about the book," he said.

"Oh," Lauren brightened with understanding. "Well, I actually do know someplace that would work, but you might think I am really trying to put pressure on you—so I almost don't want to tell you."

"Is it cooler than in this Jeep?" he asked.

"Of course, anywhere is cooler than in this Jeep," she replied.

"Just tell me, then, so we can get going." He started the Jeep. "I'm really melting here."

"Well, I thought we could go sit at my church. It's open and air-conditioned. Mutual is there tonight, so we won't be exactly alone, but we can slip into a classroom and talk."

"What's Mutual?"

"Youth group—twelve to eighteen-year-olds," she explained.

Cameron nodded. Youth groups he understood.

"Well, I think it would be okay. Lead on." He put the Jeep in gear.

The drive to Lauren's building took less than five minutes. From Cameron's point of view, the building wasn't much to look at. It was a large, one-story structure, similar in many ways to the churches he had attended in Kentucky, except this building was painted a creamy orange color that reminded him of the fifty/fifty ice cream bars he used to eat as a kid. There was a small, neatly tended lawn out front. About ten to twelve cars were parked to the side of the building, but no people were around. It was too hot to be hanging outside.

Cameron parked in the only significant shade he could find. It was a little farther from the front door but afforded his Jeep a leafy covering from a neighbor's overhanging tree. He hopped out and was at Lauren's side before she even had time to unfasten her belt.

They brought both Books of Mormon and entered through a single glass door. They went down a hall and into a foyer. The inside of the building was noticeably cooler, and about a half-dozen girls were crammed onto a small sofa laughing and giggling under a beautiful picture of Christ. A set of big, wooden double doors opened momentarily to reveal a basketball game in progress in a large gym. The plainness of the building on the outside masked the open friendliness of the inside of the building and the people it housed.

Lauren motioned for him to follow her down a hall to the left. Small windows in many of the doors lining the hallway revealed classrooms of various sizes. Lauren opened one of the doors and motioned him in. They entered a nursery, at least he thought it was a nursery. It had all the toys and toddler accoutrements, but there were no cribs. And it had that distinctive nursery smell—old baby burp mixed with ground-in graham crackers and a hint of baby wipes. The furniture consisted of a large, low table surrounded by twelve tiny chairs.

Lauren pulled out a small chair and plopped down. Cameron looked around for a larger chair and in the absence of one pulled out an equally diminutive chair. His knees were at the same level as his chest.

"Well, it's cool at least," Cameron volunteered from his low perch.

"What?" Lauren said in mock astonishment. "You don't like my pick of rooms?" Her face radiated goodness.

Cameron suddenly wondered if this had been such a good idea. Her smile was hypnotic, and he wondered how he could be sure he was being influenced by the spirit of God and not the spirit of Lauren's smile.

"No, the room is fine. The chairs are a bit small, but it's quiet and cool." He nodded his overall approval.

"We won't be bothered in here, and we can use this room until about nine or ten, depending on when they're done with basketball," Lauren said.

Cameron absently picked at a glob of glitter glue on the tabletop.

"So?" Lauren asked.

"So?" Cameron mimicked.

"Well, this is the part where you talk, or ask questions, or tell me what you thought of the book," Lauren said.

"Oh, that." Cameron's face felt a little warm.

Lauren narrowed her eyes as she looked at Cameron. "Are you blushing?"

"No," Cameron said quickly, but he knew for a fact he was. He felt shy in front of this Mormon girl for some reason. Sure, he had questions, lots of them, but being with her was getting in the way of being with her. He couldn't think straight.

"All right then, I'll start," Lauren volunteered. "What do you think so far?"

"It's different, that's for sure, But, well, I always thought it would be weird, based on what people said about it. But it isn't really weird at all. In fact, it just reads like a book of scripture," Cameron said.

"Bingo," Lauren said with a satisfied look on her face.

"Not so fast. I just said it read like scriptures, not that I believed that it was. For all I know, the Torah or the Koran may read like scripture too, although I will admit that I haven't read either of them."

"But Cameron, we're making progress." He liked the way she said his name. She drew it out ever so slightly, and it rolled off her tongue until it tickled his ears. "You can admit that it's not the horrible work of the devil that you were lead to believe it was, right?"

"Right." Cameron thought back to his reading of Third Nephi. Whatever it was, the Book of Mormon was not satanic. It had left him with the most peaceful, warm feeling. He would have read more if it hadn't gotten so late.

"So what questions do you have? You must have some," Lauren said.

Cameron exhaled deeply and replied with resignation, "Yes. Yes, I do."

For the next hour and a half, if anyone had looked into the window of the nursery, they would have seen two young people deep in conversation, conversation that was punctuated by both laughs and occasional tears on the part of the participants who were desperately seeking common ground.

At about 9:15 someone opened the nursery door.

"Oh, I'm sorry. I didn't know there was anyone in here. I was just turning out lights for the bishop." The young man's dark hazel eyes registered surprise at finding someone in the room.

The person who spoke was about Cameron's age. His voice was low and pleasant. He was professionally dressed—at least by Cameron's standards. The young man at the door had on a white shirt, conservative blue tie, and black pants. His dark, tight curly hair was cut close to his head.

"Oh, we were just leaving anyway," Lauren said as she quickly stood up from her little chair. With little warning she started to teeter toward Cameron and actually fell forward.

"What the . . . ?" Cameron said as he caught her full weight in his quickly outstretched arms.

"Whoa," Lauren said from her semi-collapsed position on Cameron. " I think I stood up too fast." She disentangled herself from Cameron and sat on the top of the table.

The young man in the doorway quickly entered the room to offer help. "Are you okay?" the white-shirted boy asked. His voice was full of concern.

"Oh, I'm fine, Elder."

Cameron took note of the fact that this kid had on a name tag: Elder Shorts.

"Should I go get the bishop?" Elder Shorts asked.

"No, really, I'm okay . . ." But before Lauren could finish her sentence, Elder Shorts was out of the room.

Less than sixty seconds later, Elder Shorts was back with an Elder Abinante. Elder Abinante had a similar severe haircut, but he was slightly shorter and rounder than Elder Shorts. Behind them both was a kindly looking, gray-haired man. The older man spoke.

"Lauren," he said in recognition. "I thought it was one of the Laurels. What's up?"

"Nothing really, Bishop. I just stood up too fast and got a little dizzy. It was probably scarier looking than it was dangerous."

The bishop nodded. "What are you two doing in here anyway?" The bishop turned his head in the direction of the two sets of open scriptures sitting on the table. "A little late for a scripture chase, don't you think?"

"Well, this is my friend Cameron." She motioned with her head toward Cameron, who was still sitting on the minuscule chair. "He's been reading the Book of Mormon, and he had a few questions." At this revelation the two elders stood straighter and visibly perked up. "He wanted to talk somewhere quiet and air-conditioned."

"Oh," the bishop said, seeming to understand. "So are you all right?"

"I'm fine, really. I just stood up too fast."

The bishop nodded again. "Well, I'm leaving in about half an hour. Why don't you sit here for a while and catch your breath. Stand up a little slower this time," he said with fatherly concern, and he turned and left the room.

"Cameron, remember I told you about my brother going on a mission next month? Well, these guys are missionaries too. This is what my brother will be doing—only in Portuguese in Brazil," Lauren said.

Cameron nodded a hello to the elders.

"I'm Elder Shorts." The taller of the two held out a hand to Cameron. He offered a firm, welcoming handshake. Elder Abinante followed suit.

"So Elders, where are you both from?" Lauren asked conversationally.

"I'm from Lansing, Michigan," Elder Shorts said.

"I from the Philippines," Elder Abinante said with a thick foreign accent and a huge white smile.

"Cameron is from North Dakota. He just moved here. Actually, he drove here—in his Jeep. Well, he originally comes from Kentucky. That's where his mom and sister still live. He lives with his grandmother in Roseville. Oh, I'll bet you know her. Sister Richards," Lauren added.

Cameron looked at Lauren. Why was she volunteering this information to these two strangers? He shook his head slightly at himself. Lauren was just nervous. He doubted if she had any ulterior motives.

"Jeep? The raised one in the parking lot?" Elder Shorts asked.

"Yeah," Cameron replied.

"Cool, but wasn't it a rough ride? I had a Jeep myself. Driving cross-country must have been hard."

"Yeah," Cameron agreed, "especially on my butt."

Elder Shorts laughed. Elder Abinante obviously didn't know the word and looked confused. Lauren pretended to look shocked.

"So, Lauren," Elder Shorts asked, "need any help in explaining stuff?"

"Well, I don't know. Cameron asked a few questions I wasn't sure about." She pulled a piece of paper from her scriptures. "I wrote them down so I could ask my dad and get back to him."

"Could we try?" Elder Shorts asked innocently.

"Cameron?" Lauren looked at Cameron.

Cameron frowned slightly. He didn't want professionally trained missionaries. He looked at Lauren hard, hoping she could read his body language, but her body language was shouting above his. The eager look on her face and the way she leaned toward him with anticipation made him squelch his initial hesitation. Letting these guys answer a few questions would clearly please Lauren, so he sighed for the millionth time tonight and motioned for the elders to take a tiny seat at the table.

When Cameron's knees finally hit the soft, nappy wool carpet next to his bed, it was 11 o'clock. He figured he had only had two, or maybe three, hours of sleep in the past few days—and that was only if you counted the nap in his Jeep at lunch today.

His prayer tonight was one of puzzlement. Every sincere question Cameron had had after reading the Book of Mormon was logically answered to his satisfaction by either Lauren or the two elders.

As he knelt beside his bed, all he could think to say to his Father in Heaven was, "what does all this mean?"

He crawled on top of his sheets and was asleep before he could even formulate a possible answer.

THURSDAY

*T*hursday morning's tickling sun rays came through the window sooner than Cameron expected them. His body and mind were still fatigued.

At breakfast his grandmother had tried valiantly to engage him in pleasant conversation, but his lack of reciprocation bordered on rudeness, and he found himself apologizing to this sweet old woman he was growing fonder of each day. He gave her a hug before he left for work. It was their first awkward attempt at physical contact between grandmother and grandson. It was just enough to make his grandmother tear up, which in turn caused a small lump to form in Cameron's throat.

At his request his grandmother didn't pack a midday meal. He had a lunch date.

Cameron's morning went slower than the past two days. The arc welder wasn't getting hot enough, and Roland finally agreed that they were going to have to call in a repair guy.

Because welding was what Cameron was hired to do and the welder was broken, Cameron had to find other things to occupy himself around the shop. He cleaned up his toolbox, reorganized his already organized work area, and was just starting to alphabetize his tools when Roland told him to take an early, long lunch. As he gathered up his things, he could see Rock standing in the bay next to him. Rock had been particularly cool toward him today and was watching him now, but Cameron didn't care. He didn't have time to deal with "Rock of my Salvation" today. He was in a great mood. He was going to see Lauren. She was meeting him before she clocked in to work.

Grateful for the extra time, Cameron hopped into his Jeep and headed to Mel's.

After being seated by Matthew and telling Brianna he was just waiting for Lauren, he got out his new Book of Mormon to read.

He was about fifteen minutes into the book when a small but powerful open hand slammed down on his book. He looked up to see the dark countenance of Rock.

Cameron was so angry he didn't even stop to think how Rock knew he was at Mel's.

"Hey, Rock, cool it!" Cameron said in a voice edged with ice.

"What are you doing, man?" Rock said with genuine, if misguided, concern.

"Reading."

"I can see that," Rock said sarcastically, " but why?"

"Because I want to," Cameron replied honestly.

"Because of the blond chick?"

"Partly," Cameron admitted.

"The Mormon." Rock spit out the word in disgust.

Cameron's face was getting red. He gripped the edge of the table with his hand and held it there to keep it steady. "Yes, she's Mormon. So are all of my relatives. I told you that yesterday."

"I know, but you also told me you'd been saved. So which is it?"

"What? It's both. I've been saved and my relatives are Mormon. It's not an either/or question. What's your problem?"

"This." Rock pointed to Cameron's Scriptures. "My problem is that I can't see you being tricked into reading this . . . this . . . " Rock inserted a pretty nasty swearword to punctuate his sentence.

Cameron could feel Matthew's and Brianna's eyes on him. The people in the next booth were equally involved in this unfolding, noisy drama now.

Cameron stood up. He was a head taller than Rock. "Rock, cool it! If you want to talk, we can go outside."

"No, man, you cool it. I just won't let these perverted Mormon freaks get to you. You have to stop reading this trash," Rock said as he slapped at Cameron's Book of Mormon again.

Cameron reached over and pulled his book off the table, closing it as he placed in on the seat of the booth.

"Rock, I am not going to have this conversation with you in here."

Rock glared at Cameron; then he leaned past Cameron and spit on the closed Book of Mormon.

In one graceful motion, Cameron's arm swung around the partially bent over Rock, and he threw him to the ground. Rock landed on his rear end. In a split second, Rock was on his feet and threw a punch that caught Cameron straight on the side of his nose. Cameron reeled backward and fell awkwardly into the booth. Before Cameron could get back up, Rock was pulling Cameron off the seat by his feet. Cameron felt, and heard, the dull thud as the back of his head hit the gray and white checkered linoleum. Cameron kicked his feet out enough to trip Rock. Rock fell on top of Cameron, angry punches flying toward Cameron's face. Cameron pulled his arm out from under the weight of Rock's body and tried to shield his head. It did little good though, and Rock only stopped when Matthew and another employee pulled Rock off of him. He lay on the floor until Brianna came over and helped him sit up. She handed him a napkin. He could feel blood running down his nose and chin. He was having a hard time breathing through his nose, so he switched to mouth breathing. His head hurt, and he reached around to feel a large, tender bump that was beginning to form.

Cameron could hear sirens in the distance.

Lauren, who was being taxied by her mom, pulled in the parking lot right behind a police car from the Roseville Police Department. As Lauren got out of the car, she heard the officer speak into his handheld unit, "Ten-ninety-seven . . . second unit has arrived at scene . . . over." Lauren wondered what was going on. Lauren's mom parked and followed her daughter.

By the time Lauren and her mother got far enough into the restaurant to see what was happening, both Rock and Cameron were sitting in separate booths with their hands behind their backs—handcuffed.

Lauren's eyes opened wide with fear and confusion. Cameron knew she was there, but he wouldn't look at her to offer any comfort. He saw her mother and slowly slid deeper into the back of the booth.

He was sick, physically. He wanted to throw up—partly because of his head injury but mostly because his agony and embarrassment were so great. He knew in his heart he had—in one blow, literally—

lost Lauren, lost his job, and probably lost his welcome by his new family as well. He doubled over in the booth, as much as was possible with his hands behind his back, to ease the nausea in his stomach.

How could he have screwed up his life so badly in such a short period of time? Tears stung his eyes. They rolled down his face and mingled with the sweat and blood near the corner of his mouth. He licked his upper lip and could feel the jagged tear in the swollen skin.

Lauren, her mother, Brianna, and Matthew huddled in a corner of the restaurant. They were talking, and Matthew was gesturing wildly. Cameron could see it was a reenactment of the fight scene. Lauren was on the phone to someone. Lauren's mom just nodded and tried to sneak peeks at Cameron when she thought he wasn't looking.

Cameron licked at his upper lip again. He could still taste the bitter salt of his own fresh blood. The police had questioned him, but he figured they had just laughed at the reason he gave for starting such a bloody fight. "Yes, officer, sir, he spit on my new scriptures." What an idiot he was. He was going to jail—he could feel it. Just as he was formulating the story he was going to have to tell his mother before he went back to Kentucky, Roland pushed his entire 350-pound frame through the door.

Cameron moaned out loud, which caused a few people to look his way. *Great*, he thought, *I'm going to be fired in front of all these people.*

Roland surveyed the scene and walked over to where Lauren and her group stood. He shook Lauren's mom's hand. He stood with the group for a few minutes and then walked over to one of the Roseville police officers. Cameron could see that he shook this guy's hand also. Roland was one likable and well-connected guy. He was going to miss working for him.

The officer had evidently given the okay for Roland to approach Cameron, because Roland was walking his way.

"Cameron, how's the nose?" Roland asked.

"It hurts and itches a little," Cameron said.

"Bill," Roland motioned toward one of the officers he was on a first name basis with, "thinks it may be broken."

"I don't know. Maybe, I guess. How's Rock? Did I hurt him?"

Roland shook his head. "Sorry, kid, you're not much of a fighter. The only blood on Rock is yours."

"Good," said Cameron. He let out an audible sigh of relief.

Roland eyed him thoughtfully. "I heard that Rock, among other things, spit on your new Book of Mormon."

Cameron met Roland's eyes for the first time. Just the way Roland had said "Book of Mormon" made Cameron pause.

"Yes, he did," Cameron said.

"So you pushed him down?"

"Yeah. I was mostly trying to get him away from my book. But I did push him down, that's true."

"What happens now?" Roland asked.

"I don't know. I guess I go to jail," Cameron said resolutely.

Roland stood up and put a beefy hand on Cameron's shoulder in a gesture of comfort. He walked back toward the officer he had been speaking to earlier.

A few moments later, Officer Bill Clark came over to Cameron. He reached behind Cameron and unlatched the metal cuffs that were restraining his arms.

Cameron rolled his shoulders backwards and forwards to ease the cramping and tension.

"Okay, kid, here's the deal," Officer Clark said as he bent down toward Cameron's face. "No charges are going to be filed—this time." The officer was quick to add. "You're lucky Roland's your boss. He vouched for you both, but *mark my words*," the officer's voice rose until everyone in the restaurant could hear him. He was actually shouting in Cameron's face now, *"If I ever find you fighting in this town again . . . "* His voice lowered to an angry whisper, and his eyes narrowed as he looked Cameron straight in the eye. He moved even closer into Cameron's personal space. Cameron could smell bacon and onion on his breath. He practically hissed. ". . . you *will* go to jail."

The officer backed up.

"Yes, sir," Cameron said sharply. He felt like saluting.

Evidently, Rock was getting the same lecture from a different officer because he heard a clear "Yes, sir" from across the restaurant.

Cameron didn't move after the officer left. He didn't know if he was free to go or not. He heard one of the officers using a microphone voice, "Four-fifteen disturbance has been mutually resolved. The combatants will be seeking their own medical attention. Ten ninety-eight, we're clearing the call now, over."

In a moment Rock walked past Cameron. His eyes were focused on the tile floor. He looked up once and winced at the sight of Cameron's face. Cameron wondered if there was a mirror somewhere.

Just about the time Cameron was thinking he could safely get up, his Uncle Mike pushed the door open and entered the restaurant. Cameron took one look at his ever kind and patient uncle and tears involuntarily filled his eyes. He lowered his head, tears of shame running down his red cheeks. He was aware that he was an embarrassment to the current Richards family—much as his father must have been years before.

His Uncle Mike walked with purpose. He wasted no time talking to Lauren's group, the police, or Cameron's boss. He came straight over to Cameron. He quickly noticed the blood, tears, and despair on Cameron's face. He gently helped him to an upright position, and then pulled Cameron tightly to his chest. Cameron leaned on his uncle for support. He had been so afraid of his disapproval and was so surprised by Mike's total and full acceptance that he laid his bloodied face on Mike's shoulder and began to sob.

"I'm so sorry, Mike," Cameron choked out, over and over again.

Mike just held him and let Cameron release all his frustrations on his shoulder. Mike waited until Cameron's breathing had evened out and then gently released his grip on his nephew.

In a short time, Cameron had calmed himself and pulled back from his uncle, slightly red with embarrassment. Cameron tried to wipe the blood from his uncle's shirt but could see it was futile.

"We need to get you to the hospital. I think your nose is broken," Mike said gently.

"I've heard." Cameron was coming to terms with this awkward piece of information. "Is it bad?" He reached up to touch it but winced at the pain.

Mike scrunched up his face a bit, trying to figure out the best way to phrase the news. "It's a little crooked, actually, but," he added quickly, "I'm sure they can straighten it out, and if not, well, just think of that Owen Wilson guy, the actor with the crooked nose. His nose is a trademark of sorts."

"That bad, huh?"

"Yeah, sort of," his uncle agreed.

Roland walked over. He put out a hand and shook Mike's. Mike took his hand and said, "Roland."

Cameron had a slightly confused look on his face.

"Roland and I go way back," Mike said simply to Cameron. To Roland he said, "This is my nephew Cameron."

Roland laughed. "We've met. He works for me."

Now it was Mike's turn to be surprised. "Really? I didn't know."

"Yeah, he and the kid he was fighting with both work for me."

Mike nodded his head in understanding. "Well, I've got to get Cameron to the E.R."

"Cameron," Roland turned to face him, "just take tomorrow off. The welder won't be fixed until Monday anyway."

Cameron looked at Roland in surprise.

"What?" Roland said. Then Roland narrowed his eyes in understanding. "You thought I was going to fire you?" Roland laughed. His big belly shook. "No way, Cameron. You are hands-down the best welder I have ever hired, and Rock lives to pick fights with Mormons. He's been doing it with me on and off for years."

Cameron looked at Roland in confusion.

"Oh, most people don't know I'm Mormon. I'm . . ." he turned to Mike for confirmation, "what do you call us now? Less active?" Roland laughed.

"Roland and I went to seminary together," Mike said in explanation.

"So do you know Lauren's mom?" Cameron asked.

"Yeah," Roland replied. "I live down the street from her. She's my wife's visiting teacher."

Cameron was too tired to ask what that meant, but that explained why Roland had been talking to her.

As normalcy was returning to the restaurant, Lauren and her mother inched closer to where Cameron, Mike, and Roland were standing. Cameron could feel Lauren as she cautiously entered his space. Her mother held back a bit.

He turned slightly to meet Lauren's approaching gaze. She gasped audibly when she saw his face up close for the first time. She tried her best to will away the tears, but they came anyway. Cameron reached over with a shaky hand and touched one cheek where the tears ran silently. Lauren reached up and wrapped her fingers around his hand where it touched her face.

"I'm supposed to be the one comforting you," Lauren said.

"You are," Cameron replied.

She gently moved his hand away from her face but didn't let go. It was an action that did not go unnoticed by her mother.

"I can't believe what that creep did to you!" Lauren said angrily.

"I started the fight, Lauren. I let him get to me."

"But he provoked you," Lauren protested.

"No matter. I swung first. I'm incredibly lucky. It could have been worse."

"How?" Lauren asked, looking directly at his crooked, bleeding nose and cut upper lip.

"I could have hurt him," Cameron said.

Lauren could see his logic, but for her part, she was proud of Cameron for defending his right to read the Book of Mormon, even if it did get physical.

"So are you going to the hospital?"

"Yeah, I guess Uncle Mike is going to take me."

"Do you want me to come? I'm pretty sure I can get the afternoon off." Lauren looked down at the floor shyly.

Cameron intertwined his fingers with hers. He closed his eyes before responding in a hoarse whisper, one word at time, "More than you will ever know."

Cameron and Mike had been in the hospital waiting room for over an hour. Lauren was not there. Her mother had thought it best if Mike took his nephew there alone. No amount of tears or bribery on Lauren's part could change the situation. It was a dismal ending to a dismal day.

Cameron shifted the ice pack covering half his face and moaned ever so slightly. The ER staff had given it to him during the triage portion of the visit. Mike looked at him and spoke. "Hurt?"

"Yeah," Cameron admitted.

"Anything I can do?" Mike asked.

"Gotta gun?" Cameron twisted his face into a half-smile and then winced.

"You don't have to talk."

"I know, but actually, if you don't mind . . ." Cameron hesitated. He had not really discussed much with his uncle since they left the restaurant. His uncle had sort of taken charge, and Cameron was just along for the ride. Not that Cameron minded, he couldn't concentrate anyway. His mind was on other things—like the Book of Mormon, Rock, and Lauren—not necessarily in that order. "Did Lauren tell you I was reading the Book of Mormon?"

"No, but your grandmother did. She called last night," Mike answered honestly.

"Oh." Cameron didn't know what to make of this information.

"She was in tears, actually."

"She often is," Cameron said observantly.

Mike nodded and continued. "She said Lauren had bought you a new set of scriptures."

"A quad," Cameron said.

Mike looked at Cameron for a moment in silence. "Right. A quad."

"Why is it called a quad if it has five books of scripture in it? Shouldn't it be called a 'quint?'" Cameron asked.

"Uh, I think because the Bible is considered one book. But, actually, now that you mention it, I suppose the Bible is two books." He paused for a moment and then finished. "I don't really know. I never thought about it till you brought it up."

"Oh, well, that's not really my big question . . ." Cameron let his words fall away casually as he thought of Lauren and her firm testimony. He then slipped back into silence.

"And?"

"What?" Cameron looked at his uncle, slightly puzzled.

"What is your big question?" his uncle said in a quiet, patient voice.

"Oh, sorry, I zoned for a minute. Umm, my question is, well, how do you know if the Book of Mormon is true? I mean really know. I know that Lauren says she knows, but it's not like you can ever know for sure."

"Well, I suppose I would have to disagree with you there. I know it's true." Mike folded the day-old *Sacramento Bee* he had been reading. He set the newspaper on the seat to the left of him and turned to face his nephew.

"But how? Is it something you feel and if so, what does it feel like?"

"That is probably the most frequent question ever asked in connection with reading the Book of Mormon, and I know this is going to sound like a weak answer, but everyone comes to the knowledge in the way that is best suited for them. Some feel a burning in their heart, some a peacefulness about them, some people just feel right about it—the truth reveals itself in increments—and some hear voices . . ."

"Voices?" Cameron looked shocked.

"Well, more of an internal voice, I suppose, and then I've heard of some who got confirmation in a dream."

"Well, to be honest, I have been feeling something, but it's hard to define, and to make it more complicated I can't decide if I am just feeling this way because of Lauren."

"How far have you read?" Mike asked.

"Somewhere in Alma."

"That's a lot of reading to do for a girl you just barely know, especially Second Nephi."

Cameron blushed. "I sort of skimmed that part. It was a little more difficult to read."

"Agreed, but still, to read all the way into Alma just for Lauren? Has it occurred to you that you may be reading it for yourself now?"

"I guess not . . ." Cameron looked out the window at a passing ambulance. "Maybe what I am feeling is real—real weird for sure—but real, and that is why I lost it with Rock. I never really thought about it that way." Cameron paused and sighed. "Mike, what really happened with my dad and his parents? I mean, I am sort of leaning toward feeling this book is true, but why didn't my dad get it? He was raised Mormon."

"I don't know the whole story. Remember, I was only about nine at the time, but I have heard from my folks that your dad was always fairly rebellious. I only remember your grandmother crying at every holiday after he left, and then your mom started sending pictures of you and Caitlin and it probably saved her life. Your grandfather was more stoic. He never said much, but your dad leaving tore him up inside."

"Do you think it's a coincidence I'm here, that I met Lauren when I did?"

Mike eyed Cameron carefully before he spoke. "No."

"Neither does Lauren. She seems to think it is all part of some cosmic plan."

"Do you have a problem with being part of a larger 'plan'?" Mike asked.

"Maybe." Cameron wiped at his chin where drops of water were beginning to form from the condensation on his ice pack. "I suppose it would depend on whose plan it was."

"Good answer. So whose plan would you be agreeable to following?"

"Uh . . . Christ's?"

"So if you knew this was the course that Christ would want you to follow, then you might be more willing to give up a little control to him?"

"I suppose, when you put it that way, but how do you give up control of something you don't have control of in the first place?" Cameron asked.

Before Mike could respond, they both heard Cameron's name being called out by a male nurse.

As it turned out, Cameron's nose wasn't actually broken—at least not in the technical sense of the word. The cartilage was bent, but under the expert hands of the on-call orthopedic doctor, his nose was gently realigned, swaddled in bandages, and cooled some more with squishy blue ice packs. Unfortunately, around his eyes the rapidly expanding shadows of pooled blood testified of the force of impact Rock's fist had had on his face.

He looked as miserable as he felt, but his current misery wasn't physical. The doctor had given him something for the pain and swelling, and the ice packs had helped too. His current pain was strictly emotional. When Lauren's mother had not allowed her to accompany him, she said it was because she didn't want Lauren to get in the way. But Cameron was sure there was more to it than that. He figured that up until the scene at Mel's, Lauren's mother had, for the most part, been unaware of him. Now she was acutely aware. Cameron had noticed how she had raised her eyebrows when he had touched Lauren's face and then subsequently taken her hand in the restaurant.

Cameron's stomach rumbled loudly enough for his uncle to look his way. They had been in the hospital for almost four hours. He was starving. He was supposed to have met Lauren for lunch, and lunch was long past.

"How much longer do you suppose?" Cameron asked.

"Hungry?" Mike said.

"Starving, actually." Cameron's stomached rumbled again in agreement.

"I think we're almost done. Can you eat?"

"Well, I can talk. Not to say I can't feel it, but I am hungrier than I am in pain."

"Do you want to go out?" Mike asked.

"No way. I've had it up to here with restaurants in California. No, I just want to go home."

"Home? Back to Kentucky?"

Cameron turned to face his uncle more fully. "No, home. Gramma's."

Mike just nodded.

～～～

Cameron's grandmother had been pacing the floor in his absence. The woolen carpet she vacuumed each day had a distinct pattern of newly crushed wear. As he pulled up in front of the house, and before he had even gotten out of his Jeep, he could see her through the windows, walking back and forth. They had gone back to Mel's to pick up his Jeep, and now his Jeep and Mike's truck were parked together in front of the small house.

His grandmother gasped when he walked in behind Mike. "Oh, Cameron," she said in a quiet, high voice as both hands raised to her cheeks. She looked older today.

Cameron blushed and his face was even more mottled and distressed looking. He hadn't realized how awkward seeing his grandmother was going to be. What must she think? He wondered if he reminded her of his father.

"Gramma, I am so sorry. I . . ." He didn't know what to say, so his words just hung in the air.

I what? he thought. *I didn't mean to get hit after I hit someone? I didn't mean to get angry? Or the real question, I didn't mean to be like my father?*

His grandmother looked slightly surprised at his apology.

"Sorry for what? Lauren said that boy started the fight and hit you."

Cameron shrugged his shoulders. "She makes it sound so noble."

"She said you were defending the Book of Mormon," his grandmother continued.

"Well, I wasn't exactly defending the book, Gramma. Maybe my right to read it, but, well . . ." He turned to Mike for some sort of support, and to his surprise, his uncle spoke.

"Cameron is reading it, but it's hard for him, Aunt Clara. Not the reading part, but the part where you aren't sure of what you're feeling. I gather he didn't want us to know he was even reading it, so this whole thing is a little awkward for him. I think we need to give him some time and space." Cameron was amazed that his uncle could so easily articulate what he was feeling.

His grandmother looked to Cameron for confirmation, and he nodded weakly.

"Well, that's fine. Of course that's fine. So what did the doctor say?" she said, changing the subject back to the more physical aspects. She was looking directly at his bandaged nose.

Mike answered for Cameron again. "The bone is not broken. He *will* be better before he looks better."

Cameron managed a weak smile.

"Are you hungry? Can you eat?" his grandmother asked.

"Yes and yes, but I think I need something a little soft."

"Enchiladas?" His grandmother smiled sweetly.

"Uh . . ." Cameron hesitated until he saw the big grin on his grandmother's face. She had just made a joke.

"What would you like, honey?" she said when she saw he got her attempt at humor.

"Soup?" Cameron asked.

"Soup, we have. Anything else? Mike?"

"Nothing for me, thank you. I have to get back to the store."

Cameron hadn't really thought about his uncle having taken off work. His uncle turned to leave, and Cameron followed him out the door and onto the steps.

"Uncle Mike," Cameron said as he looked off toward some imaginary thing to the left of his uncle, "thank you."

Mike put his hand on Cameron's shoulder and squeezed it.

"Cameron, remember when you asked how you give up control of something you don't have control over?"

Cameron nodded. Indeed, Cameron remembered. For some odd reason, it was all he had thought about since they had left the hospital. His life was reeling out of control, and he didn't know how to stop it.

"I think when you are feeling out of control, that is the best time to let someone take over, and who better than your Heavenly Father?"

"But how? How does that happen?" Cameron asked.

"You have to ask for help. You pray, don't you?"

"Yes, of course."

"Then ask. You've read James 1:5, I'm sure: 'If any of you lack wisdom, let him ask of God, that giveth to all *men* liberally, and upbraideth not; and it shall be given him.' You just need to ask. Heavenly Father will take care of the rest."

"So you're saying, I just ask for Heavenly Father to take control?"

"Yes."

"How do I know when I get an answer?"

Mike smiled. "I'm pretty sure you'll know. Just listen with your heart." He squeezed Cameron's shoulder one more time, dropped his hand, and walked to his truck.

Cameron stood on the porch and watched as his uncle got in his truck and drove away. He couldn't help thinking what a difference there was between his uncle and his father, and it made him a little sad at what might have been. He turned and walked into the house.

The house was cool and welcoming. His grandmother had a bowl of chicken noodle soup on the table along with sliced watermelon. He sat down and started to pick up the spoon but then stopped.

"Would you like me to pray, Gramma?"

Clara seemed slightly startled but nodded.

"Father who art in Heaven, thank you for this meal. Thank you for all you have given me in Roseville, especially my new relatives and friends. Help me to live up to their expectations and bless this food. In Jesus' name, Amen." Cameron smiled shyly at his grandmother and put a spoonful of the hot liquid and squishy noodles in his mouth. It was just the right temperature, not too hot and not lukewarm. He could eat it fast, which he did.

There was no conversation as he ate his food. His grandmother had come over to sit across the table from him. She watched him, but surprisingly it didn't make him nervous—it seemed natural and loving.

When he was done, she took the bowl and refilled it.

He ate some more. As it turned out, he ate two full cans of soup. His stomach was finally quiet.

"Lauren called," Clara said.

"Oh?" He tried not to sound excited, but the catch in his voice might have given him away. "Did she say anything?"

"Well, actually, yes. She told me about the fight and then I told her I would have you call her when you got home, but she said specifically not to have you call her. She said she would call you at eight o'clock tonight."

"Oh." Cameron wondered why he wasn't to call her. Then he remembered that he only had her home number, and the subject of their last conversation. Her mother had been there. It wasn't pretty. Of course, he thought, it could be nothing more than that she was still at work and wouldn't be home till then. He glanced at the clock on the stove. Either way, it didn't matter. It was almost eight o'clock anyway.

No sooner had he thought this than the phone rang. They both looked at it, and his grandmother got up and answered it by the third ring. She said hello and then handed it to Cameron.

"Hey, Cameron," Caitlin said.

"Hey to you too." It was nice to hear his sister's voice.

"Mom's at the movies and won't be home till late, so I am sort of sneaking in a phone call. How are you?"

"Uh, fine," Cameron lied. He didn't want to tell his sister about his broken nose.

"So did you get a job?" Caitlin asked.

"Yeah, actually I did. I work for a nice guy welding on trucks and stuff."

"Is it full time?"

"Yeah."

"So you have to work tomorrow?"

"Uh, no, actually the welder broke. So I sort of have the day off."

"Cameron?"

"Yeah?"

"What's up?"

"What do you mean?" Cameron said slowly.

"You know darn well what I mean. You're holding back something. What's up?" Caitlin insisted.

There was no use lying to Caitlin. She knew him too well. She had always sensed when something was bothering him. He realized that Lauren had that same uncanny knack.

"Well, okay, something happened, but don't you dare tell Mom, and I mean it."

"Yeah? Okay."

"I sort of got in a fight with a kid at my new job and got my nose bent."

"What? You got your nose broken?"

"Not broken. Not exactly, just bent a little. It's fine. The doctor at the E.R. just pushed it back in place. It looks like . . . " He started to say "hell" but then looked at his grandmother, who was listening intently. "H. E. double toothpicks."

Caitlin laughed on the other end of the line. "H.E. double toothpicks?"

"Shut up, Caitlin. Anyway, it's not that bad. It looks way worse. But the part about the welder being broken is true, and before you ask, no, I didn't get fired. Me and this kid just got into a heated discussion over something."

"What? You haven't been there that long. What could you possibly get into an argument about?"

"The Book of Mormon, actually, but like I said, don't you dare tell any of this to Mom."

Caitlin was quiet for a moment. "No, of course I won't. You can trust me."

Cameron looked at the clock again. It was almost eight. "Hey, I have to go. Call me tomorrow if you can. I'll tell you more, okay?"

"Okay," Caitlin said, and with that she hung up.

Cameron handed the phone back to his grandmother, who put it on the wall unit. Her hand barely pulled away from the phone when it rang again. She picked it up on the first ring.

"Hello? Yes. He's here." Clara handed the phone to Cameron again.

"Hello?"

"Hi," Lauren whispered into his ear.

"Why are you whispering?" Cameron asked.

"Because I don't want my mom to know I'm on the phone. She's not real happy right now, and I don't want to make things worse. But I had to talk to you to see how you are."

"Is she upset because of me?"

"Well, she's more upset because of *me and you*." Lauren's voice was soft, and Cameron had to strain to hear her.

"Why?"

"Remember I told you I didn't date nonmembers?"

"Of course, but you said that you were okay with it now," Cameron said, confused.

"I am. I'm okay with it. Really. Unfortunately, my parents aren't."

"So are you saying we can't go out?" Cameron could feel his chest getting tight.

"Worse than that," Lauren admitted. "They are forbidding me to see you at all."

"But why? Just because I'm not Mormon?"

"Well, it's a little more complicated than that."

"So, uncomplicate it, Lauren. You can't . . . well, I mean . . . " He looked up at his grandmother, and she immediately understood his desire for privacy. She quietly walked out of the room. He heard her bedroom door shut and was grateful she was not as intrusive as Lauren's mom seemed to be.

"Listen, Cameron, I am not saying I am going along with this plan, but I do see where they are coming from," Lauren said.

"Where?"

"Remember I told you I have a two-year-old nephew?"

"Yeah, your brother's son."

"My younger brother's son. My eighteen-year-old brother's son. The girl was not Mormon."

"Oh," Cameron said slowly. He was beginning to understand. He didn't like it one bit, but now he could see why her mom was so into her life. This actually did explain a lot.

"But your parents can't honestly think we would . . . or that you would ever . . . " He didn't finish the sentences, but they both knew what he meant.

"Apparently, they do. Did you know that's why I don't drive?"

"What does driving have to do with getting pregnant?"

"My brother's girlfriend was a little older than my brother, and her parents had bought her a car for her sixteenth birthday. They used to go everywhere in that little car. Evidently, that is where she and my brother had . . . well, you know."

"What kind of car?"

"A Volkswagen Beetle," Lauren said.

"What? No way. I think that's impossible," Cameron said practically.

"Obviously not. Anyway, I guess my parents figured if I didn't have access to a car, that would keep me out of trouble."

"So your parents don't actually hate me. They just don't want us driving around together?" Cameron asked hopefully.

"Nope. Right now they pretty much hate you," Lauren said.

"Great. So what are we supposed to do?"

"I don't know. I am working on it."

"How?"

Lauren was quiet for a moment, but a sweet stillness filled Cameron as she said, "Praying, of course."

Lauren's voice suddenly got louder. "So anyway, Stacy, I think going to the mall tomorrow is a great idea."

"Is Stacy there?" Cameron asked.

"No," Lauren said.

"Are you talking to me?" Cameron asked again.

"Yes," Lauren said into the phone.

"But Stacy is not there?"

"No, Stacy. I told you, I am not going to see him anymore, so going to the mall is fine. I don't work until five tomorrow, so we can go at one. Will you pick me up, or should I have Cale drive me?"

"Is your mom in the room?"

"Not really," Lauren said. "Well, I can ask him right now, he's standing here."

Cameron was trying to figure out this game they were playing, but it was made harder by the recent smack to his head.

"So are you saying Cale is in your room and you want to meet at the mall tomorrow?"

"Bingo, Stacy," Lauren said.

"Where do you want to meet?"

"Perfect then. I'll have Cale drop me off at Sears. Just meet me in the tool department."

"Oh, good idea."

"And Stacy, bring that book I loaned you on Wednesday."

"What book?" Cameron asked.

"You know," Lauren prompted.

"The Book of Mormon?"

"Right. Hey, I have to go, my mom wants me. I'll see you tomorrow at one, okay?"

"Sure. I'll be there. Are you going to get in trouble for this?"

"I might," Lauren answered honestly.

FRIDAY

*C*ameron woke up and looked at the clock on his nightstand. The red digital numbers glowed: 4:26. He needed his medication.

He padded into the quiet of the kitchen and found the prescription his uncle had picked up at the hospital pharmacy. His whole body ached now, not just his head and nose. He washed two pain pills down with a tall glass of ice-cold milk. It felt good as it ran down the back of his throat and spread fingers of cold into his stomach. He breathed in deeply and drank the rest of it in one swallow.

Outside the small window over the sink, dawn was approaching from the east. Little pink clouds licked at the sky on the horizon. Maybe clouds were a good thing. Maybe it wouldn't be so hot today.

He headed back toward his bedroom and slumber. He had read in his Book of Mormon until one o'clock in the morning. He was almost done. He didn't need to be up until noon, so he fully intended to sleep all morning. He walked past the sewing/guest room on the way to his bed. The door was open, and he could see more pictures of him and Caitlin. When he got up, he would look at these and maybe see if his grandmother had a picture album of his father.

He didn't fall asleep right away. He hurt and the medicine had not kicked in yet, but gradually his breathing relaxed. His last thoughts were of Lauren the Mormon and her wondrous "Golden Bible."

When he became aware again, he could feel someone running their fingers gently over his head. He was still under the influence of the pain medication and struggled toward consciousness. He thought maybe it was his grandmother, because he was awake enough to know it wasn't Lauren. Whenever Lauren was around, he could feel her, and he knew she wasn't here in his room. He moaned slightly as he turned to face whoever was sitting on the side of his bed and was startled to see his mother.

"Mom?"

"Hey, Cameron." His mother's face was soft with concern.

"What the . . . what are you doing here?" Cameron asked. He looked around to get his bearings. Yes, he was in his room in Roseville. Yes, his mother from Kentucky was sitting on the side of his bed, in Roseville. He shook his head slightly but then immediately regretted it as a wave of pain shot through it. His face crumpled with the effort. His mother saw it and laid her hand lightly on his chest. He spoke again. "How did you get here? What are you doing here?"

"We took a red-eye from Louisville. I came because I heard you got in a fight at work and broke your nose."

"It's not broken, and I told Caitlin not to tell you. Wait . . . did you say we?" Cameron asked.

"Yes." His mother smiled.

"Caitlin's here too?"

"Yes. She's in the front room looking at pictures with your grandmother."

"I still don't understand. What about your job? How did you get the time off? When did you call in? Won't you get in trouble?"

"Calm down, Cameron. The store can get along fine without me for a week. I called in this morning from the airport. I told them I had a family emergency in California. What are they going to do, fire me?"

Cameron shrugged. "They could."

"They won't. I'm the best checker they have and they know it. It's fine. You didn't think I was going to just sit at home and worry about you, did you?"

"No, and that is why I told Caitlin to keep her big mouth shut," Cameron said with annoyance, though he was just blustering. He was so glad to see his mother that he was almost in tears.

"So tell me what happened. I'm getting conflicting stories from Caitlin and your grandmother."

"Oh, mom. So much has happened since I've been here. I can't believe it's only been a week. It seems like a lifetime ago that I was in North Dakota."

Cameron closed his eyes as he began to relate the week's events. By the time he was finished with his rendition, he was sitting up in bed with the sheets pulled around him for privacy.

"So let me get this straight. In just five days, you have managed to fall in love, be converted to Mormonism, and break your nose defending your new religion?" Cathy asked incredulously.

Cameron looked at his mother in awe. In one sentence she had completely defined what had happened in the last week. It was so clear—he was in love, he did believe the Book of Mormon was true, and, yes, he had defended it by force.

"Yep, that about sums it up," Cameron agreed.

"So what are you going to do next week?" his mother asked in all seriousness.

Cameron started to laugh. He laughed until tears formed in his eyes and started to trickle down his cheeks. His mother watched him in amazement and then his mother began to laugh too. They both sat on the bed and laughed. Caitlin and his grandmother came in to see what was so funny.

"Hey, Caitlin," Cameron said between gasps of breath.

Caitlin looked from Cameron to her mother. "What's so doggone funny?" she demanded.

"Your brother was just telling me about his week," Cathy said.

"Well, I didn't think his week was so funny. He broke his nose in a fight, Mom. What's so funny about that?"

"You had to be there," Cameron said. He was beginning to calm down, and he put his arms out to his sister. She came over, and he leaned forward to give her a big hug.

"You look awful," Caitlin said.

"I know," Cameron admitted.

"Gramma," Cameron looked at his father's mother and smiled, "it's true, isn't it?" He motioned toward the book on his nightstand. His mother and sister followed his gaze.

Clara looked at the book and then at him. She bit her lower lip and tears welled in her eyes as she nodded in agreement.

Cameron just nodded in return. "Okay, then, it's going to be a great day."

"I was just making some breakfast for your mom and Caitlin. Do you want to eat?" his grandmother asked Cameron.

"That would be wonderful. I am starving." He looked at his mother and sister. "So where are you staying?"

"Well, we were going to get a hotel room, but Clara invited us to stay here."

Cameron looked at his grandmother. "Good idea. They can have my room, and I'll sleep in the guest room."

"Well," Clara said slowly, "I was going to have them stay in my room, and I was going to sleep in the guest room."

"Absolutely not, Gramma. No more arguments from you," he said teasingly. "I'm in the guest room, and they get to stay in Dad's old room."

"This is Dad's old room?" Caitlin asked in wonderment.

"Yeah, but Uncle Mike and his family fixed it up before I got here."

"Wow. It's kind of weird, huh?" Caitlin said.

"It was at first, but now it's just home," Cameron said.

After breakfast was over, Cameron's mom wanted to take a nap. It was almost noon, so Cameron cleaned himself up so he could meet Lauren at one. Then he quickly made his bed so his mother could nap. His grandmother went in behind him and changed the sheets—*such a grandmotherly thing to do*, he thought. His mother was soon fast asleep in his bed. He smiled at the image of her curled on the top of his covers. She looked a little vulnerable, and he felt a wave of love sweep over him. He walked into the front room where Caitlin was sitting on the couch watching TV.

"Caitlin, are you tired, or do you want to do something?" Cameron asked.

"Are you kidding? I'm wide awake. Good grief, I'm in California. I want to see it all while I can. I can sleep anytime in Kentucky."

"I am meeting someone at the mall at one. We can go now and hang out if you want."

"Yeah." Caitlin got up from the couch and walked toward the front window. "I see you still have that old green Jeep."

"What's the matter with my Jeep?" Cameron asked defensively.

"Nothing, I'm just never going to drive one. No air," Caitlin said.

"Since when did you care about air-conditioning?"

"Since I started going out with guys who could afford it," Caitlin said.

"Going out? Aren't you a little young to be going out?" Cameron said, a little annoyed at this revelation.

"What are you talking about? I'm fifteen. I'm plenty old enough to date. When did you start?" she retorted.

"I didn't date much in high school," Cameron had to admit.

"Oh yeah, I forgot. You were too busy working on your Jeep." She laughed and her laugh was genuine. "Well, I do, and Mom lets me."

"Well, okay, but be careful."

Caitlin scrunched her face into a smirk. "Be careful. You sound like Mom." She walked over to the couch and got a brown macramé string bag. She threw it over her shoulder. "Let's go already."

Cameron grabbed his keys at the same time his grandmother walked into the room. He walked over and kissed her on the cheek. "We're going to the mall. We'll be back in a couple of hours."

They got in the Jeep, and Cameron had barely pulled away from the house when Caitlin reached in her purse and pulled out a pack of cigarettes. She was reaching for the matches when Cameron spoke. "When did you start smoking?"

"Oh, a while ago. I sort of started in junior high, but that was just mostly after dances and stuff."

"And now?"

"Well, now I smoke," she said matter-of-factly. She looked at the sour expression on her brother's face. "What? You smoke."

"I quit," Cameron said evenly.

"Oh. Well, good for you." She shrugged and lit her cigarette.

Cameron wasn't going to stop her. There wasn't anything he could say one way or another that was going to make a difference. Caitlin sort of did what she wanted, when she wanted. It had always been that way. He was sure his mother did know, and while she wouldn't have approved, she wouldn't have done much to stop it.

"You can't smoke in the mall." He glanced her way to see her reaction.

"Why not?" she said somewhat taken aback.

"I don't know. Some law in California. They don't let you smoke in public places. So not at work, not in the malls, not in restaurants."

"Not in restaurants? That sounds stupid," Caitlin observed. She took another long drag on her cigarette.

Cameron was slightly surprised to find he didn't like the smell of her smoke drifting his way. He was glad they were in an open Jeep.

"Did I mention that we're going to be meeting up with my girlfriend?" Cameron said.

"Girlfriend? How could you have a girlfriend in just five days?" Caitlin asked.

Cameron just shrugged again.

"What's she like?"

"Oh, you'll like her. She's really nice, very pretty, and *very* Mormon."

"Mormon? You're dating a Mormon girl? I thought you got in a fight because you didn't like Mormons."

"Who said that?" Cameron asked in amazement.

"Mom did," Caitlin said.

"Actually, I'm glad you brought Mom up. Why did you tell her about my nose and the fight?"

"I didn't want to. Honestly. She was in the house when I was talking to you. I didn't know she had heard me until I hung up. She made me tell her everything."

"So just what did you tell her?"

"Nothing. Just what you'd said—that you had gotten into a fight with some guy over the Book of Mormon and that you broke your nose."

"I didn't break it. It's just bent," Cameron said, annoyed at his sister.

"Bent. Broke. Same thing. You got in a fight and got your nose bent, whatever. Anyway, she got all wiggy and flipped out. She kept saying it was her fault. She said we were going to go to California. Hey, I wasn't going to stop her. If she wanted to take me to California, I wanted to go. So we went to the airport and got on a plane."

"But that must have cost her a fortune," Cameron protested.

Caitlin shrugged. "I don't know. She used a credit card."

"Je-ma-nights," Cameron said as he turned into the mall parking lot. "I'm going to have to repay her. She doesn't have money for trips to California."

Caitlin just shrugged.

As Caitlin got out of the Jeep, she threw her cigarette down and ground it out with her sandal. Cameron got out and grabbed his Book of Mormon as Lauren had requested. Cameron waited until Caitlin was done putting out her cigarette; then they both walked toward the entrance to Sears.

"So what are Mormons like?" Caitlin asked sincerely.

"Most of the ones I've met are really nice. All of the family on the Richards side is Mormon. The kids I've met are pretty much like the ones at our churches. They pray, go to church on Sundays, and read scriptures."

"That a Book of Mormon?" Caitlin asked as she looked at the book Cameron was carrying.

"Yeah," Cameron replied.

"So what did you mean when you asked Grandmother Clara if it was true? Were you talking about the Book of Mormon?"

Cameron stepped up on the curb and onto the sidewalk. "Yeah."

"So you think the Book of Mormon is true?" Caitlin asked in amazement.

"Yeah, I do," Cameron said honestly.

"How could you possibly know that in five days?"

"Well, for starters, I read it."

"When?"

"I started Wednesday and I'm almost done. I only have one more section to go."

"So you read the book, and just like that you know it's true?"

"Yep."

Caitlin shook her head in disgust. "Oh my gosh, Cameron. What have you been smoking out here? That is the dumbest thing I've ever heard. Did it ever occur to you that Satan is working on you?"

Cameron sighed. It had only been a few days since he was saying the same thing.

"Look, it might be better if we don't discuss this right now, okay. Yes, I read the book; yes, I believe it; yes, I'm going to join the Mormon Church."

"*What?*" Caitlin's voice raised a full octave.

"Calm down. I'll be happy to discuss this with you, little sister, but not right now. Let's just go in and look at the mall, okay?"

Caitlin narrowed her eyes and took a step back from Cameron. "You're scaring me now, Cameron."

They entered through the big double doors of Sears and passed through the store. Soon they were out into the center section of the mall. Caitlin was visibly impressed and didn't say anything more about the Church or the Book of Mormon.

"Hey, this is cool. This is bigger than that mall in Louisville. Oh my gosh, Abercrombie and Fitch," Caitlin said as she scurried over to inspect a wall-sized picture of a half-naked guy in a pair of cutoff jeans. He had a well-developed chest, and if his jeans had been any lower on his hips, it would have been porn.

"Let's go in here." Caitlin grabbed Cameron by the hand and pulled him into the store.

As it turned out, it was probably a good store to be in, given how tired he was. He got to sit on a chair while his sister tried on every pair of short shorts in the store. She had brought some of her babysitting money with her, and she evidently planned on spending all of it today. He kept glancing at his watch. At 12:50 he told Caitlin to wrap it up, to either to buy something or go get dressed. She went and got dressed. Obviously, there was more fun in trying on clothes than in actually buying them.

They walked back down the center of the mall and turned toward Sears.

Lauren was standing in front of the toolboxes when Caitlin and Cameron walked up. She was visibly taken aback when she saw Caitlin. Caitlin's long dark hair was pulled back into a ponytail that cascaded in curls down her back. Her clear, dark eyes were staring straight into Lauren's. She smiled and her teeth were straight but slightly yellowed, which surprised Lauren. Without being told, she knew this was Cameron's sister.

Lauren extended a hand toward the girl as she came closer. "Caitlin, I presume?"

"Yeah. You must be . . . hey," she turned to Cameron, "you didn't tell me your girlfriend's name."

"Lauren," Cameron said. "This is Lauren."

"Oh. Well, how do you do, Lauren? I'm Cameron's sister."

"I can see that. You look a lot like Cameron."

"Yuck. I hope not." She glanced at her brother and squinted her nose.

"No. I meant you have his coloring and similar hair and eyes. You are clearly a very beautiful version of the Richards side of the family," Lauren said, trying to backpedal.

"Well, I don't know. I don't know many of my Richards relatives. I only just met my grandmother this morning."

"My mom and Caitlin decided to come and surprise me in California. They took a plane out last night and got to my grandmother's this morning about ten," Cameron said by way of explanation. He was hoping that Lauren would hold off on the questions until they were alone for a while.

"Oh," Lauren said, still somewhat confused at the whole situation. She was just barely prepared to deal with Cameron this morning, and a little sister just added to her stress. She sniffed the air and noticed the smell of stale cigarette smoke. Cameron? Or was it the little sister?

"So, Caitlin still wants to try on clothes. I thought you and I could just go to the food court and talk, if that's okay with both of you," Cameron said.

"I like that plan," Caitlin said. She looked at her watch. "It's one o'clock now. How about I meet you at two?"

Cameron was surprised that Caitlin was so eager to leave, but then the mall was calling to her, so he shrugged his shoulders.

"You don't, by chance, have a cell phone, do you, Cameron?" Caitlin asked.

"No, too expensive," Cameron said, and then he paused. "Don't you dare tell me that you have a cell phone."

Caitlin reached into her purse and pulled one out. She held it up for Cameron to see.

"Where did you get that?" Cameron demanded in his older, wiser brother voice.

"Mom bought it for me for my birthday." Caitlin tilted her head and smiled sweetly at her brother.

"Uh," Cameron stammered.

"I have a cell phone," Lauren said. She reached into her purse and pulled hers out. "What's your number and I'll put it in mine."

Lauren and Caitlin exchanged numbers. Then Caitlin rushed into the mall.

As soon as Caitlin was out of sight, Cameron pulled Lauren behind the largest tool chest in the store. He put his Book of Mormon on the empty chest. He looked around them and then, deciding they were relatively alone, wrapped his arms around her waist and pulled her into him. He bent down to kiss her full on. At first she held back, startled, but then she relaxed and kissed him back—losing awareness of the retail surroundings. A Sears employee walked by but completely ignored this sudden burst of passion in the tool aisle.

When Cameron pulled away, he smiled. His bandages crinkled as the corners of his mouth turned up in a grin.

"What?" Lauren said. "You look like that Cheshire cat from *Alice in Wonderland*."

"It's true," Cameron said.

"It's true? It's true that you look like a Cheshire cat?"

He slowly shook his head. "No. It's true," he repeated simply.

"What's true?" Suddenly, her face lit up. "Oh my gosh, Cameron. Cameron, are you saying what I think you're saying?"

He smiled his answer. She threw her arms around his neck and began to kiss the sides of his face. Carefully and sweetly, she kissed him all over his face and neck. When she kissed his ears, he shuddered and put both of his hands on her face and slowly backed her away.

"Uh, we might want to go to the food court now."

Lauren just smiled. "Okay, if you say so."

Cameron took her hand in one hand and grabbed his book in the other.

"Does your sister smoke?" Lauren asked as they were walking by the kiosks.

"Yeah." Cameron let out a big breath.

"That old Kentucky thing?"

"I suppose. I started when I was her age. I don't know that I can do anything about it."

"Oh, I know. Younger siblings can be a pain-in-the-rear."

"Speaking of pain-in-the-rear siblings, tell me more about your brother and this kid of his."

"Well, David is eighteen. He graduated in June. He is supposed to go to Sierra College in the fall. He wants to be a fireman. His son is Devin, and he is absolutely the most adorable little boy in the world. Our whole family loves him to death."

"So who takes care of him?" Cameron asked.

"My brother, when he's home, my mom, when he isn't. My brother works right now at a gas station."

"I didn't know that," Cameron said. He was surprised to find he and this brother had something in common.

"There is clearly more you don't know about me than what you do know."

"If I never knew one more thing about you, Lauren, I know all I need to know to love you for the rest of my life."

Lauren looked down at the pink ceramic tile of the mall floor and walked forward in awkward silence.

"What?" Cameron asked, but he knew he had gone a sentence too far.

"Cameron, don't say anymore. This is hard enough already."

Cameron could feel his heart start to quicken in his chest. His hand began to sweat immediately, and he wanted to pull away from Lauren. He didn't want to hear what she had to say next. He wanted to put his hands over his ears and run out the nearest exit.

He started to pull his hand away, and Lauren gripped it tighter. "You are not going to run. You have to hear me out."

He turned his head away from her. "I don't want to," he said plaintively.

"First, answer me this: Is the Book of Mormon true?" Lauren said.

"Yes."

"Is it true because of me?"

"No," he had to admit.

"So what I am about to say won't change that, will it?"

"Lauren, I can't do this." He tugged his hand away from hers.

"You have to, you have to hear me out . . . because . . . because . . . I'm in love with you."

Cameron turned his head back toward her. This was the last thing he expected her to say. He had thought she was going to tell him to get lost, that she couldn't date a non-Mormon. How could she say she loved him now? What kind of a cruel joke was she playing on him?

"I don't understand," he finally said.

"You and me both," Lauren admitted honestly.

"The way you were talking made me think you were leaving," Cameron said.

"I am."

"You're leaving?" Cameron asked, his mind trying to process all that was being said.

"Yes. You know I'm leaving. I'm supposed to go to BYU in three weeks, but now . . . " Lauren's voice cracked, and she couldn't finish her sentence because little girl sobs began to tear at her body.

"What? What's the matter?" Cameron found himself getting panicked once again.

"My parents are sending me to Utah early. They're sending me to my aunt's in Orem tomorrow."

"Oh, please tell me you're kidding," Cameron pleaded.

"I wish I was, but the thing is, Cameron, I do love you. I don't know why, or how it happened, but it did. I couldn't leave without telling you in person."

Cameron's head hurt so badly now that the throbbing was getting in the way of rational thought.

"Well, what are we going to do?" he said at last.

"I sort of had an idea. You may think it's crazy, but it's all I could come up with after praying and reading the scriptures. Oh, and now I know what you mean about wondering what is the Spirit and what is the influence of love. Anyway . . ." She paused to make sure she had Cameron's full attention.

He nodded. "Yes?"

"Well, why don't you apply to BYU? You could come up in the winter. You said you would have liked to go to college. So do it. Do it now."

"Lauren, I would like nothing more than to go to college, and to be where you are is an even more powerful incentive, but I don't have the money."

"So borrow it," Lauren said simply.

"From whom? Who do I know who has . . . " He looked at Lauren, and it dawned on him where she was going with this conversation. "Mike?"

"Why not? It would just be a loan. He's your uncle. I know he has it. At least I am pretty sure he does. Stacy is a bit of a chatterbox sometimes. I know they have enough to send all their kids."

"I couldn't just ask Mike for the money, Lauren. There is no way I could do that."

"So don't ask Mike, ask Heavenly Father."

Cameron thought back to what Mike had said less than twenty-four hours earlier: "If any of you lack wisdom, let him ask of God . . ."

"Well, I could pray about it."

"Do you love me, Cameron?" Lauren asked.

"You know I do," Cameron said simply.

"Then you'll be worth the wait."

Cameron looked down at his CTR ring and then at Lauren's CTR ring. He reached over to her hand and gently tugged at her ring.

"What?" Lauren protested slightly as he took the ring off of her finger.

"Come with me." He took her by her hand and walked back toward Sears. Before they reached the large department store, Cameron turned into the jewelry store.

He went to the woman at the counter and held out the ring. "Do you engrave rings?"

"Yes," she said.

"Can I get it done now?"

The woman looked toward the back of the store. There was a man behind a glass counter at a workbench. He was reading a magazine. "I think so. How many letters?"

Cameron did a mental calculation. "Uh . . . twelve."

"That will be twelve dollars plus tax."

"Great." He pulled his wallet out of his back pocket and put thirteen dollars on the counter. Then he placed the ring on top of the cash. "I would like you to engrave on the inside band of this ring: WORTH THE WAIT."

Caitlin met back up with Lauren and Cameron at two o'clock. Caitlin had the faint smell of fresh cigarette smoke, which both Cameron and Lauren chose to ignore. She had two bags of clothes with her, one from Wet Seal and the other from PAC SUN—clothing stores known for their hip, trendy style.

"So what did you guys do?" Caitlin asked.

"Just walked and talked mostly," Cameron said.

"Mom is probably up. We'd better get back, don't you think?" Caitlin said.

Cameron did *not* want to leave, but he knew it was inevitable. "Yeah, you're right."

"Can I hitch a ride to Mel's? I'll just hang out there for a while before work."

"You start at five, right?" Cameron said.

"Yeah," Lauren replied.

"Well, come home with us. Meet my mom. I sort of told her all about you."

Lauren pulled back from him a little. "Is that a good thing?"

"For sure, it's a good thing. My mom is really pretty cool. In fact, if it weren't for my mom, it may have taken me much longer to figure out what happened to me this week. She pretty much summed it up in one sentence," Cameron said.

"Which was?" Lauren asked.

"Uh, well . . . " Cameron looked at his little sister and didn't want to go on.

"Hey, I want to know too," Caitlin said.

Lauren shook her head at him. He was not going to be able to escape now. He had started, and now, between his sister and Lauren, he was trapped.

"Well, she said I fell in love, converted to Mormonism, and broke my nose."

"Smart mom," Lauren said.

"What was so hard about that?" Caitlin asked.

"Your brother has a difficult time with simple, human communication," Lauren explained for Cameron.

"Tell me about it," Caitlin laughed.

"All right. I'll come home to meet your mom, but I have to be at work by five," Lauren said.

"Agreed," Cameron said, and they all walked out of the mall.

The weather had turned and instead of the blast furnace of the past few days, a temperate, humid breeze washed from west to east across the parking lot. There was the faintest smell of smoke in the air.

"What's that smell?" Caitlin asked.

"Probably a brush fire somewhere. When the weather gets like this," Lauren pointed at the dark clouds that flitted across the sky, "we get a lot of dry lightning. It's fire season right now."

"But they don't get in the city, do they?" Caitlin asked somewhat concerned.

"No, but sometimes they do get in the foothills. Hey, this is California. We're known for our 'shake and bake' weather." Lauren laughed at the old regional joke.

"Shake and bake?" Cameron asked.

"Sure. Earthquakes and fires," Lauren said.

"That sounds bad. I didn't know you had earthquakes this far north," Caitlin said.

"Sure we do, but I'll admit, not like in southern California."

"Oh, I'd hate living here then. Earthquakes, yuck," Caitlin shuddered.

"And I suppose tornadoes are better?" Lauren asked.

"Well, at least you know they're coming," Cameron said defensively.

"That's not what I hear," Caitlin said. Just then the low rumble of thunder vibrated through the parking lot. One car alarm, obviously set too sensitively, started to howl.

Running and laughing, they reached the Jeep as the first big raindrops started to fall. Caitlin knew to get in the back. Lauren got in next to Cameron. He only had a standard bikini top on his Jeep, so by the time they got home Caitlin was soaked. She didn't seem to mind, though.

Cameron sent the girls inside while he pulled out the soft top to his Jeep. It took him ten minutes to get it on, but he finally zipped the last of the zippers and raced up the steps. It was really coming down now. He was as wet as Caitlin. *Well, at least this rain should help with the fires,* he thought. Cameron opened the door to hear his grandmother say, "Broken nose."

"Hey, how many times do I have to tell you guys, my nose is not broken? It's just bent."

The four of them stopped, looked at him, and then burst out laughing.

"What? It's not broken."

"Cameron, believe it or not, not everything that is said in this house is about you. Your grandmother was talking about your grandfather," his mother said.

"What?" Cameron said, unsure of himself and wanting to exit and reenter, to try again.

"Cameron, I was just telling your mom and the girls about the time your grandfather got his nose broken, and his was broken—not bent," Clara said.

"Grandfather Richards?"

"Yes, it was on his mission. His story was not nearly so exciting as your story though. He just had a door slammed in his face, and he didn't step back in time. I actually met him the next day. His nose was crooked and his eyes were black and blue, just like yours are today. Such a sorry sight. Can you believe I fell in love with that?" His grandmother laughed at the sweet memory. She pointed at a very old picture of a very young man. "If you look really closely, you can see his nose is crooked."

Cameron, Lauren, and Caitlin walked over to the fireplace mantle to inspect the picture more closely.

"Hey, you can see it. How funny," Caitlin said. "Why did someone slam a door in his face?"

"Oh, he was on his mission and back then people were not so accommodating of Mormon missionaries."

"You mean those guys who ride around on bikes in white shirts and ties everywhere?" Caitlin asked.

"Yes," Clara said.

"How did you know that?" Cameron asked. Up until he had met the missionaries on Wednesday night, he hadn't even known Mormon missionaries existed.

"They're all over, Cameron. I can't believe you didn't know that," Caitlin said.

Lauren smiled sweetly at Cameron in an "I told you so" manner.

"So basically, Brother Richards was on his mission, standing up for his beliefs, and he got his nose broken?" Lauren said to Cameron's grandmother.

"Yes," Clara said. The irony of the situation did not escape anyone but Caitlin.

"Sister Richards, did you or Brother Richards go to college?"

Cameron gave Lauren a quick don't-go-there look. She looked right back at him and smiled sweetly.

"We both did. BYU, actually."

"You did?" Cameron said in amazement.

"Yes. Your grandfather was an engineer, and I got my teaching degree."

"I thought you said you lived here most of your life," Cameron continued, a little confused.

"I did, but it was after we went to school. Your grandfather's parents paid his way, and I went on a partial scholarship and worked part time."

"Did you know Cameron had a 3.9 GPA in high school?" Lauren asked Clara.

"No," she looked at Cameron, "I didn't."

"Oh, that's nothing. He got a perfect score on his ACT," his mother added.

"What?" Now Lauren was the one to be surprised.

"Mom!"

His mother shrugged her shoulders in response.

"Why didn't you go to college then, Cameron?" his grandmother asked him directly.

"Uh . . ."

"I'd like to hear this too," his mother said.

"Uh," he stammered. "I . . . well, I just . . . I don't know," he finally said.

His mother took over for him. "I think I know. He didn't think we could afford it, and for some reason he was too proud to go asking for scholarship money."

"Pride goeth before the fall," Caitlin said dramatically.

"Oh, don't you start quoting scriptures to me now," Cameron said to his sister, and all the women in the room started to laugh.

"So it was about the money?" Clara said directly to Cameron.

"Well, sort of. Listen, the thing my mom and Lauren here didn't tell you was that I took a bunch of auto classes. My GPA is more a reflection of that. I'm not some genius boy."

"I'll say," Caitlin added to be helpful.

"All right, I'll accept that," his grandmother said, "but a perfect score on the ACT's is a little harder to sweep under the carpet."

"I'll say." This time it was Lauren who chimed in.

"If you could have gone to college, what would you have done?" Clara asked. She sounded very much like his high school guidance counselor.

"Teach, I think, though I know realistically it doesn't pay real well," Cameron added, "The reason I took so many auto classes was because of my teacher. He helped me out at a time in my life when things weren't going so well for me. It left a big impression on me." He looked at his mom and saw sad remembrance in her eyes.

"I loved teaching," Clara said wistfully.

"But hey, I like working with cars too," he said, trying to lighten the mood. "My boss is nice."

"Yeah, and the people you work with are real peaches too," Lauren added sarcastically.

"Oh yeah, the kid you got in a fight with works with you, huh?" Caitlin said.

"I was just telling Cameron this afternoon that he ought to consider going to BYU," Lauren said.

"Oh really?" his grandmother said. "And what did he say to that?"

Cameron was annoyed that his life was being diced and sliced by these females right before his eyes. *Maybe,* he thought, *I should just leave the room, and when I get back, they will have it all neatly packaged for me—maybe with a nice bow on it.*

"He said it was a good idea but that he didn't have the money."

Thanks, Lauren, he thought to himself, but didn't say a word out loud.

"Oh, but he does," said his grandmother. "He's had a college fund since he was one. So do you Caitlin."

At this, Cathy gasped and then burst into tears, as mothers often do.

Cameron just looked at his grandmother. "What are you saying, Gramma?" He watched his mother stand and walk toward the bathroom—to get tissues, no doubt.

166

"When you were born, I rolled your father's college fund into an account in your name. I think there is about $50,000 in there now. It might be more." She shrugged her shoulders.

Cameron reached out for the back of the chair next to him. Lauren came over to his side and took his hand. It was shaking.

"I can go to college?" he asked incredulously.

"If you want to," his grandmother answered.

"When?" he asked.

"Whenever you want to."

"Now? Like this semester?" Cameron was still reeling.

"Well, there are some colleges you can go to this semester if you want. BYU is not one of them. You have to apply, and that takes a while."

"So, let me get this straight. I can go to college and not work and just be a student?"

"Yes." His grandmother was being very patient with him.

His mother had returned to the room, carrying a wad of toilet tissue. The tears were still flowing.

Cameron took in a deep chestful of air and then said with finality, "Then I will."

Cameron pulled into Mel's ten minutes before five. He went around to Lauren's side and helped her out. He leaned against the backside of the Jeep, and Lauren stood facing him.

"So this isn't it, is it?" she asked tentatively, her eyes lowered so she wouldn't look at him and cry.

"Oh, heck no." He wrapped his arms around her and held her tight to keep her from tearing up. It had the opposite effect. She started to cry.

"What are we going to do?" she whispered into his ear. The softness of her breath caught him off guard, and he momentarily lost his courage. All he wanted to do was pick her up, put her in his Jeep, and run far, far away with her. He was twenty-one, she was nineteen. It could work. People had eloped before. He shook the feeling and pushed her away from him, ever so slowly.

He put his finger under her chin and raised her head. He had to maneuver a little to get her to look him in the eyes, but when he did, he wouldn't let her gaze go. "You keep praying and I will too. I just know this is not how it ends."

"Okay," she said.

He wiped the tears on her cheeks away with his thumbs. "You are so beautiful. You know that, don't you?"

Lauren blushed.

"Even more so when you blush like that." Cameron touched the tip of her nose with his finger.

"Are you going to get baptized?"

"Is that how you join your church?" Cameron asked.

Lauren laughed. There was so much he didn't know yet. "Yes."

"Then, yes, I'm going to get baptized. Do you sprinkle, or do you guys do the whole dunk thing?" he asked, ever practical.

"Uh, we dunk."

"Oh, okay, that works too," Cameron said.

"Do you think you can find some excuse to come and have an ice cream tonight?" Lauren asked.

"Of course, and I don't really need an excuse." He pulled her back into him and held her tighter than before.

"Okay, well, I've got to go." She said the words, but her feet didn't move.

"Yeah, I know," he agreed, and kept his arms around her.

She rested her head on his shoulder. "I don't want to go in."

"I know."

"Can't we just run away together?" she asked.

Cameron jumped a little. He had never said a word about this to Lauren. Was she reading his mind, or were they just so connected that they thought on a parallel plane?

"No, we can't."

"Oh. Well, okay," she said with resignation. She put both hands on Cameron's chest and pushed away from him.

Cameron watched her walk away. She waved from inside the restaurant, and he got back in his Jeep. He pulled out of the parking lot and turned right. He drove toward his Uncle Mike's.

Mike was out front working on a sprinkler when Cameron pulled in. He looked up from the mud hole he had created and smiled at his young cousin.

"Well, this is a surprise. Where's your mom and sister?" Mike asked.

"Back at the house. I needed to talk to you alone," Cameron paused, "if it's okay."

"Of course it's okay. Do you want to go inside?" Mike motioned with his head toward the house.

Cameron looked toward the house and thought of all the kids inside. "No. This is good."

"Okay. What's up?"

"Well, I've had a pretty busy week."

Mike laughed. "That would be an understatement."

"And now I've got a serious problem. I have prayed about it, and I felt like I should come and talk to you."

Mike nodded his head very bishop-like and didn't say a word.

"So here's the deal, in a nutshell: I'm in love with Lauren. I read the Book of Mormon, and I know it's true. I know I am going to join the Mormon Church, although at this point I am not sure just how that works. Lauren's parents hate me and are sending Lauren to Utah tomorrow to live with an aunt or something to get her away from me. And, oh yeah, my grandmother is sending me to college."

"Wow, Cameron, that's pretty impressive."

"What, all the stuff that has happened to me in one week?"

"No, that you could say all those sentences without taking a breath. You might consider choir."

Cameron looked at his uncle, not knowing how to respond.

"It was a joke, Cameron," Mike said.

"Oh." Cameron was so stressed out that he didn't get his uncle's form of humor.

"Anyway. Let's try and break this down into more manageable pieces. What was the first one?"

"I'm in love with Lauren."

"Stacy's friend?"

"Yeah."

"Good choice," Mike said.

"Her parents hate me, and they are sending her away tomorrow to live in Utah."

"I didn't think you had had that much contact with them."

"I haven't. I haven't even met them, actually. Well, I saw her mom—twice. And one of the times I was in handcuffs."

"Oh yeah. Well, that would be a little disconcerting for even the most liberal of parents. Is that why you think they hate you and are sending Lauren away?" Mike asked.

"Well, that and Lauren said it had to do with her brother and his son."

"Oh. Well, I can see that too."

"So you agree?"

"I didn't say that. I just know where they're coming from. They're scared Cameron. They're just trying to protect Lauren. You can understand that, can't you?"

"Maybe. It might be easier to understand if I wasn't the one they were trying to protect her from."

"Understood. Well, what do you think you should do?"

"I don't know. That's why I came over here. I thought you might have some ideas."

"Nope, not really. But if you tell me some of yours, I'll see if any of them sound reasonable."

Cameron didn't understand why his uncle was working him so hard.

"Well, I sort of thought maybe if I talked to them . . .?" He said this as a question because he wasn't confident enough to come right out and say that this was a workable plan.

"Okay, any more ideas?"

"Well . . . "

"What? Lay them all on the table, so we can sort them out."

"Well, I have to admit I did consider either kidnapping or elopement."

"Now there's two ideas that will really make points with her parents."

"Okay, so I know those two aren't the greatest ideas, but that's all I've come up with so far, and oh, to come over and talk to you."

"Oh, I like this last one the best." Mike smiled broadly. "But, let's go back to the first one."

"The one where I talk to her parents?"

"Yeah, that one. What if you took someone with you, someone who could vouch for your good character?"

"Like Roland?"

"Well, sure, Roland might work, but I was thinking of someone else."

"My grandmother? They don't even know my grandmother."

"You're getting warm, Cameron. Who do you know, who they already know, who knows what a great kid you are?"

Cameron shook his head in bewilderment.

Mike started to make peddling motions with his hands and said, "Sounds like . . . "

"Bike?"

Mike nodded his head.

Cameron suddenly rolled his eyes and dipped his head down in embarrassment. "You? You would go with me?" He tripped, ever so slightly, over the words.

"Of course I would."

"But when? She's leaving tomorrow."

Mike stood up and said, "Well, I guess I'd better go change into my official advocate clothing."

Cameron looked puzzled again. "A joke?"

Mike smiled. "Yes, a joke. I must be losing my touch. Let me go change out of these work clothes. No use my getting dirt on their clean sofas. We *are* trying to put our best foot forward."

On the ride over in Mike's truck, Mike and Cameron discussed how one went about joining the Church. It was decided that Mike would baptize Cameron after he had had the discussions but that he would have the discussions in an accelerated fashion so he could be "dunked" next Saturday.

As far as college was concerned, they discussed a few options. One option was to go to Sierra College, which was local and cheap. His uncle thought it might be the best route to get him back in the groove of studying and then he could apply for BYU. Assuming his grades were similar to those he got in high school, his uncle assured him that getting into the Y would not be a problem.

But there was another option: he could go straight to Utah and go to a community college there. That way he would be near Lauren, but that would take more doing because he would have to move, find an apartment, and leave his new network of friends and family.

His third option was to go to most any college of his choice. His uncle stressed that BYU was not for the fainthearted, and while he had read the Book of Mormon, he might be overwhelmed by the whole cultural shock of living in Provo, Utah, where being Mormon had been become an art form.

Mike parked across the street from Lauren's home and turned off the engine.

"Scared?"

"Petrified," Cameron admitted.

"So what would you normally do in a situation like this?"

"Honestly?"

"Sure."

"Run."

"Okay, what's your second choice?"

"Pray."

"Ah, good choice. Why don't we do that, then?"

After a simple but powerful prayer by Mike, they went up to the front door and knocked.

Lauren's parents were expecting them. Mike had called ahead. The living room was quiet. There was a television on in another part of the house, but it wasn't on loud enough to tell whether it was the news or cartoons.

"Mike," Lauren's dad said and offered his hand to Cameron's uncle. "Come in."

Lauren's mother held back, as did Cameron. He was so nervous that he felt like throwing up, but he just kept repeating under his breath, "Father in Heaven, help me, please."

They all sat down—Lauren's parents on the couch, Cameron and Mike on chairs facing them.

After they were seated, Mike took the lead. "Cameron has a story he would like to tell you, and I think it is a story you need to hear."

Lauren's parents just nodded and looked at the shaking, pale young man with black eyes and a bandaged nose sitting on their chair.

Cameron started at the beginning, back in Fargo where he first found the ring. He hadn't rehearsed what he was going to say, but it came out coherently and with real emotion. When he got to the part where he had stayed up until 4:30 in the morning to read their daughter's Book of Mormon, Lauren's mother was biting her lower lip. By the time he had finished with the fight scene, Lauren's father was reaching for his wife's hand. They were somewhat taken aback to find out that Lauren had gone to meet him at the mall, but they let go of their parental annoyance when they found out about Cameron's upcoming baptism. By the end of the tale, Cameron was surprised to see that Lauren's mother was openly crying.

The evening ended with Cameron being assured that Lauren, while she would be going to BYU for the fall semester, would not have to travel the next day to her aunt's in Utah. A great burden was lifted from Cameron's heart. Lauren's parents promised that they would be at his baptism the following Saturday. They were beaming in the role their daughter had played in bringing Cameron back to his family *and his God.*

Cameron walked into Mel's diner and caught the eye of the evening hostess. On her nametag was a neatly typed "Lauren."

She smiled shyly and said, "Hi, how many?"

"Just one. Nonsmoking, please," Cameron said.

"We only have nonsmoking here, sir," Lauren replied.

"So I've heard. You get off pretty soon, don't you?" he asked the pretty girl with the emerald green eyes.

"Sir, while that may be true, we are not allowed to date customers."

Cameron laughed. "So that's going to be your excuse tonight?"

"Whatever works." She winked at him and then turned to walk him to their booth.

"Your parents said I could take you home tonight," he said from behind her.

Lauren stopped and he almost ran into her back. She turned to face him and spoke. "Cameron Thomas Richards, don't you dare tease me like that. Not tonight, of all nights." She almost burst into tears.

"Well, if you don't believe me, ask them." He pointed toward the window that had an open view of the parking lot. Standing at the window were her mother, father, brothers, and nephew, and right behind them were Cameron's mother, Caitlin, and his grandmother. They all raised their hands to wave at the surprised hostess.

"What does this mean?" Lauren said with genuine confusion in her voice.

"It means . . ." Cameron took Lauren's hand and placed it like a bookend on his hand. He then intertwined his fingers with hers until the CTR rings were touching. "It means that coming here was definitely 'worth the drive.'"

EPILOGUE

August 11, the night before Cameron was baptized, the heavens were ablaze with falling stars. Cameron and Lauren sat on Mike's back deck and tried to count them, but the later it got, the more rapidly they came—a shower of radiance that spread across the eastern sky.

Words like *wondrous* and *glorious* could not describe either the heavens or how the young couple were feeling. In the morning Cameron would be taking his first official step toward membership in Christ's church. He was both in awe and humbled at this opportunity he was being given.

In his uncle's home, at that very moment, were relatives whom he had only met tonight—relatives who had come from all over the western United States to see him, Cameron Thomas Richards, be baptized into the Church of his fathers.

Cameron had enrolled in Sierra College the previous week and was helping Lauren pack to leave for the Y. He promised to follow in January. In the meantime, just knowing that they were going to be there for each other, they could relax as Lauren's departure crept closer.

When Cameron had told Roland of his plans to attend school full time, Roland was understandably upset, but was consoled by the fact that he still had the use of Cameron's welding skills on Tuesdays and Thursdays until January.

Cathy and Caitlin Richards had sat in on the missionary discussions with Cameron. Elders Shorts and Abinante made the most of their time with the family. In the end Cathy and Caitlin had not made the commitment to be baptized, but they had admitted they felt something that neither of them could easily explain away. Cameron's mother said she would at least try to read this book they kept talking about and took her husband's old seminary set.

Clara Richards had never been happier. The older woman flitted around taking care of her daughter-in-law and granddaughter until Cathy Richards rebelled and sat Clara down with a year's supply of scrapbooking materials and told her she expected all the loose baby pictures of her late husband to be in a book by the end of the week.

About the Author

Melissa Ann Aylstock received an associate's degree in 1988 from El Camino College in Torrance, California. She has continued to attend community colleges ever since, taking courses ranging from human anatomy to construction technology.

In 1989, Melissa founded Klinefelter Syndrome and Associates, a medical nonprofit support organization. She served as executive director of the organization until December 2004, when she resigned to pursue a career as a full-time writer. *CTR's Ring* is her first novel.

Melissa lives in Loomis, California, with her husband, Roger, and one of their four children. She has been a worker in the Oakland California Temple since 2003. Melissa, who enjoys comments from her readers, can be e-mailed from her website at www.melissaaylstock.com